BACK TO THE LEGION

The Brotherhood of Tormented Men is comprised of individuals who were prisoners, tortured in the underground cells of secret police in a dozen Arab countries. On a mission, they have crossed continents to rendezvous in the middle of the Sahara. When a travel-stained group of ex-legionnaires comes upon them, that mission should spell death to the men of the Foreign Legion. But death comes to men who accept it, and these legionnaires are fighters who refuse to accept death . . .

GORDON LANDSBOROUGH

BACK TO
THE LEGION

Complete and Unabridged

LINFORD
Leicester

First published in Great Britain

First Linford Edition
published 2012

British Library CIP Data

Landsborough, Gordon.
  Back to the Legion. - -
  (Linford mystery library)
  1. Suspense fiction.
  2. Large type books.
  I. Title II. Series
  823.9'14–dc23

  ISBN 978–1–4448–1294–7

Published by
F. A. Thorpe (Publishing)
Anstey, Leicestershire

Set by Words & Graphics Ltd.
Anstey, Leicestershire
Printed and bound in Great Britain by
T. J. International Ltd., Padstow, Cornwall

This book is printed on acid-free paper

1

Dying Thirst

Suleiman the Hideous was dying. More, in moments through his increasing delirium he knew it. Death was near to him; within hours now there would be no more Suleiman, no more pain and torment for a man who had spent the last years of his life in suffering.

An expert was about to die, he thought once, cynically, in a rare moment of lucidity. A man who knew more about torture than anyone else in the world was about to go out on a rack of pain designed by Nature.

For dying by thirst is more intolerable than any man-made torture.

There was no strength left in his limbs now — hadn't been for two hours or more, and even then there'd been sufficient only to keep him staggering along over the scorching sandy wastes. But his eyes could open; he could see — and there was nothing to see.

Only sand, mound upon mound stretching to a broken horizon that suggested distant mountain peaks. Grey-yellow sand that reflected the fierce, burning Sahara sun and sent air currents rising in shimmering waves that distorted the vision.

Suleiman moaned, his mouth agape in that face that was a terror to women and children and chilling even to men used to unlovely male features. His tongue was a lump of swollen, purple flesh that protruded between his broad, flat, spade-like teeth. His eyes were nearly closed, gummed together by the incessant heat.

He was a huddle of dirty-white, ragged *galabier*, that nightgown-like garment of the *fellahin*, a knitted skullcap on his head. His last coherent thought was: 'If anyone did come by, they would not stop for Suleiman the Hideous.' For he knew how unlovely he looked.

Then he opened his eyes again — opened them that fraction of an inch that he was able. He saw, and knew that madness had come to him, and he moaned at the thought.

For he was surrounded by horsemen.

One moment the desert had been deserted of all life save himself; now when he looked there were many.

Many? He strained his bloodshot eyes, and figures merged so that there were not as many as he had thought. About six. Then delirium claimed him, for among these horsemen were Franks who wore the blue uniforms of the hated French Foreign Legion. He knew his mind had turned, and no longer did he try to control his babbling tongue.

One got down. He stood over Suleiman, staring in horror at that distorted face. He listened. It was hard to tell what Suleiman was saying, with that mouth full of swollen tongue. But finally he understood, and then he turned to his companions and said, incredulously:

'This Ay-rab's a Scotchman!'

Pure Highland Scottish was issuing through the cracked lips of the delirious Arab. The big man in legionnaire's uniform knelt by the ragged bundle on the hot sand and listened.

Suleiman the Hideous was talking about the Brotherhood of Tormented Men . . .

Suleiman found water pouring down his dry throat. There was a moment when it seemed that the liquid was being lost in his desiccated frame, like a river that runs out in the parched desert sands. And then the miracle of life asserted itself. Strength came to him; the swelling tides of torture began to recede as his clamouring body found the moisture it must have.

His head lifted, his mouth opened wider to drink greedily of that stream of warm, tasteless water. He gulped, choking, and the water poured over his lips and chin and down his hairy chest. It was heavenly, all the same.

His eyes focused on the face near to his own. That big legionnaire's. The biggest man in the party. He saw a man lean to the point of thinness, with a face almost blackened by long exposure to this merciless sun. Squinting against the light, he sought to see the man behind those grim hard features. Suleiman was thinking: 'This man is too hard. He has the face of a fighter, and there is no softness in him.' Sometimes he could approve of fighting faces, but there were times when, for his survival, it was necessary that mercy should be in the souls of the men he met. Just now was one of them.

He opened his eyes still further, searching into that face. And then he was satisfied. There *was* compassion behind those grim features.

Suleiman drank again, his eyes wandering. He saw another legionnaire immediately behind the man who was helping him. This was a different type of man — big and hulking, with ears that sat close against the skull, and a nose that seemed to have been shoved back into the broad, high-cheekboned face. The face of a fighter also, but a different kind of fighting man. This legionnaire had had experience in the boxing ring — by the look of that good-tempered face, he'd taken plenty of thrashings.

A third legionnaire was holding the horses. A good-looking, younger man. He had a redness to his cheeks showing even under the thick Sahara tan. Somehow he had the air of a schoolboy — British variety, thought Suleiman. Ripe red cheeks . . . bright blue eyes . . . But not British . . .

Suleiman's strength left him for a few minutes. The big legionnaire poured more water into the mouth, then squinted against the long rays of the descending sun towards the distant mountains.

A girl asked, urgently: 'Aren't we wasting time, Tex?'

He was shocked. 'Wastin' time?' Like the girl, his voice was richly American. 'The heck, Nicky, we cain't leave this fellar to die.'

She made an impatient gesture, from her saddle. 'I didn't mean that.' Her blue eyes dropped to that hideously, pitiable hulk on the hot sand. She gulped, and seemed to withdraw into herself. 'I mean, can't we put him on a horse and get moving?'

She, too, looked behind her towards those purple-red hills west of them, and there was fear in her lovely blue eyes. She lifted a hand to push back her straggling hair, blonde and lovely even now in its disorderliness. Her hand was trembling, as if she hadn't recovered from a recent bad experience.

Ex-Legionnaire Tex sighed. 'I figger he needs rest, not exercise, right now. Guess it might be too much for him, lyin' across a hoss in this heat.'

An Arab swung down from his mount and stood over the unconscious Suleiman. He was tall, finely made, with hands that were unsullied by work. A patrician, handsome and intelligent. His chin was curiously white, as if a beard had recently been shaved off.

He looked down at Suleiman, his face filled with contempt. 'He is a dog,' he declared in the clipped, rather high-pitched English of the educated Arab. 'The desert is full of these. His death matters not compared with what will befall us if we are overtaken. Let us go on.'

Ex-Legionnaire Tex said, politely: 'Brother, there's nothin' keepin' you. Keep goin', if you want to.'

That good-tempered, flat, battered pan on the second legionnaire cracked open. A curiously metallic voice clipped out words — 'We don't go an' leave a guy to rot in a desert. No, sir, that ain't in our vo-cab-u-lary.' He looked proud when he brought out the last word and waited for the applause. It didn't come.

The third legionnaire said: 'You quit usin' words you don't know what they mean.' Then he looked at the lean legionnaire on his knees beside Suleiman and said, simply: 'We don't go without him, huh?'

'We don't go without him.' Tex stood up. His white issue drill pants were soiled from long days on the desert; his blue tunic was ragged and stained. He shoved back his kepi, with its neck curtain, and stared yet again to the west of them. He seemed reassured, then glanced at his long shadow as if to measure the time. 'We don't need to worry. Them *partizans* won't catch up on us afore dark. Reckon we might as well camp here for the night as anywhere. By mornin' this fellar'll be strong enough to ride with us.'

He looked at that hideous, swollen face and wondered. It didn't seem possible that this *thing* could ever recover from

8

this awful, desert ordeal and be a man again. Tex had seen thirst in the desert before, but never had its effects been like this.

Then the big legionnaire caught a glint from the inert man's eye. The desert wanderer had come back from unconsciousness again and was watching him — must have understood that expression of horror on the lean American's face.

Tex heard that Scottish voice whisper: 'Don't worry ... I look like this always.'

There was even a note of humour in that cracked voice. Then the light went out of the eye again, the tongue was silenced, and Tex knew the man was unconscious.

He lowered him gently on to the sand, then stood up, mechanically dusting the knees of his pants. He said: 'Goldarn it, what d'you know? An Ay-rab that speaks like a Scotchman!' He crossed to his horse, shaking his head like a man who can see no light on an intriguing problem.

When Suleiman came slowly back to consciousness again, there was a coolness over the land. Night was approaching; the sun had gone down and the light was fading rapidly.

He stared vacantly for a few seconds, then remembered — remembered much, anyway. Instantly suspicion sent his muscles tautening, for he was a man who had lived only by the quickness of his suspicions, these many years.

He felt better, as if a lot of water had been poured into him, but over his body was that awful weariness that follows long thirst — as if he had been beaten all over.

He saw his new companions grouped together a few yards from him. Four legionnaires, he now realised.

And then his eyes became intent. For there was something unusual about that fourth legionary. For one thing, he was no ordinary legionnaire but an officer. Another, upon his head was the *kafir* and agal, that headdress of the desert nomad.

The last curious difference was that he was hobbled about the ankles, though his hands were free.

The apple-cheeked, bright-looking legionnaire was squatting opposite the Legion officer, his Lebel rifle in a position to

10

cover the prisoner if he made the slightest hostile move.

Suleiman wondered at it, wondered that legionnaires should hold captive a superior officer. For legionnaires had little love for their leaders, and a bullet in the head would have been more understandable than those cords around the man's legs.

Covertly he studied that face under the sand-dusted *kafir*. It was a thin, small, expressionless face, somehow colourless in spite of the browning effect of the fierce Sahara sun. The face of a clerk, and an unimportant clerk at that, Suleiman thought, looking at the rimless eyeglasses that gave a prissy, almost cissy, appearance to the man.

Yet this clerkish fellow was an officer in the Legion. For that reason, he couldn't be a cissy. The Legion bred men, strong men — oft-times bad, evil men — but never cissies. So appearances lied in this man's case, Suleiman knew, and it made him speculate on the reason for the officer's captivity.

Suleiman's eyes travelled round. Saw

again that big, lean, tough-jawed American. Saw the good-natured, battered face of the ex-prize-fighter legionnaire. Looked upon an Arab, dignified, simply but richly robed — obviously of the family of sheiks . . . a man who had lately lost his beard, judging by the whiteness of his jaw.

Then his heart stood still. He looked fully into the face of an Arab girl.

The girl had moved up softly behind him, had stooped to look into his face and had seen him with his eyes open. Suleiman saw big brown eyes that were as soft as any desert gazelle's. Saw smooth-rounded, honey-brown cheekbones, and parted red lips that revealed the gleaming whiteness of strong, healthy young teeth within.

A vision of loveliness, unexpected here in the desert. His eyes widened.

Then it happened as it always happened.

He saw the soft, brown eyes widen, the mouth contort in horror. He saw the girl go stumbling back as if in shock. Then she turned and ran — ran into the arms of the younger, beardless Arab.

Suleiman let his heavy lids fall, so that the vision was obscured. He sighed, the sigh of a man who has been through it all before.

And he thought: 'Truly I am named Suleiman the Hideous.' He had no illusions about his appearance. From those days in the depths of that prison in Cairo he had been a man apart because of what they had done to his face. Until now it had mattered little: sometimes it seemed that he welcomed this evidence that he was one of the Brotherhood of Tormented Men.

But now ... for a moment ... he weakened. He wanted. Wanted a girl — a woman — a wife, like other men. For he was still young and human, and he had the desires of other men, for all that no woman would look at him.

His eyes opened very slightly. He saw that vision of dusky loveliness; She was watching him, fascinated, from a distance, but it was the fascination of repulsion, he knew.

'Mahfra,' someone called, and the Arab maiden turned her head.

'Mahfra,' Suleiman repeated. That was her name. 'Rain-in-Early-Summer.' Truly a good name to give a girl who lived in the desert . . .

Suleiman the Hideous slept, while all through Arabia, through Egypt and North Africa, his brethren of the Brotherhood of Tormented Men planned towards the end that he had set out to achieve but had so far failed to accomplish.

2

Noble blood

Suleiman slept under the stars and in the coolness that night brought so that the world of the desert would have strength to meet another day's sun.

He was in a fever, a delirium, and shouted much in his sleep, but it was incoherent and made sense to no one except that tall, slow-speaking infidel with an American accent. He sat near to Suleiman's head and bathed it occasionally and sometimes poured water down the thirsting throat. He did it with thoroughness of a man who is used to more strenuous things, yet there was a tenderness behind his actions.

The others watched him, wondering that he should find such compassion for a desert wanderer, filthier and more hideous than any they had ever encountered. And they respected him, admired him because of his humanity.

That is, all but the beardless Arab. Such conduct was beyond his understanding. Weren't the desert lands full of beggars crying out for succour? By Allah, if a man gave his time to nursing the weak and fallen, he would assuredly find his hands full.

He raised the point about water in a rather peremptory tone. 'This sponge from the gutters of Tripoli has already absorbed the water of six of us for one whole day. If more is poured down that unworthy throat, there will be insufficient to take us to the next waterhole, and then we will die of thirst in the desert.'

For answer, the American stayed the clamouring tongue of the rambling Suleiman with further water from his goatskin water-container. Laconically he said: 'We'll face that tomorrow. Meanwhile, this poor devil won't live unless he gets more water pumped into him.'

There was a murmur of agreement from the other two legionnaires. The prisoner remained silent. The sheik withdrew with dignity, wrapped himself in his robes and went to sleep on the warm sand.

The blonde American girl came and sat by the big fellow. The soft night wind blew a tendril of hair across her face. She pushed it back into position, looked at Suleiman and then at the stars.

She whispered: 'What did they do to him to make him look like that?'

'They?' Somewhere a desert fox yapped and then was silent.

'He wasn't born like that. Couldn't have been. It must have been done to him.' She shuddered. 'I don't know how you can sit by him, Tex. I — I can't. He's too . . . hideous.' Then she seemed to break down for a second. 'This is a cruel land, Tex. They don't respect human life at all.'

Ex-Legionnaire Texas put one arm about her shoulders, comfortingly. 'You've had enough for one day, honey,' he told her. 'More than enough.' He cast his mind back to the terrors of the past many hours, of their nearness to savage death. But all he could say was: 'Lie down and sleep, Nicky. We'll need all our strength tomorrow.'

She obeyed. He was the leader, and though he said things quietly, gently, he had a manner that secured him obedience. But she curled up where she was, right at the heels of the big, grim legionnaire from Texas, as if alone in him she felt safety.

For an hour more Texas continued to wet the lips of the once-more delirious Arab, trying to help him, to make him more comfortable, and to get him off to sleep. In the end he succeeded, but while Suleiman's ravings lasted he learned of the horrors that had made him the man he was.

That babbling tongue told of men who followed him always, who sought to take him and put him in a quiet place where they could wreak their will on him. It told of frantic efforts to escape, of succeeding, though always in peril of his life. Of the merciless hunt being taken up again . . .

'Eyes, eyes!' moaned Suleiman. 'Always they watch, always they're staring. They're in the darkness . . . coming . . . closer . . . watching . . .'

His voice was high with the hysteria of

delirium. The big, tough-faced man who had once been a cowboy on the wide range of Texas, bent over him and said: 'You don't need to worry, brother. There ain't no eyes hereabouts — ain't nothin' to hurt you while I'm aroun', so go to sleep.' — talking to the sick Arab like a man talks to a child.

But now was the full moment of Suleiman's ravings. The Texan knew Arabic and could follow it well, though it was the Arabic of the Nile Delta and not the Bedouin tongue. In time he was able to understand the nightmare that tortured Suleiman's fevered brain.

Once again Suleiman was in Egypt. Once again he was living through that moment when he should have died but had lived. It was in the Citadel, in the catacomb prison of the Egyptian secret political police.

He was in that cold, dank, noisome cell, in a world of darkness where day followed night and the lost souls in that evil labyrinth of torment never knew of their passing.

There were the times when men's

heavy boots tramped down the echoing corridors, bringing him sweating to his feet, waiting in terror, wondering if it was his turn. Times when he heard massive doors slam back against unyielding stone walls. Times when he heard the screams of unknown prisoners as things were done to them . . . and often the laughter of the men who tore the life out of their victims.

When that happened, when they heard a brother in distress, the cells came to life — those cells that all knew were about them, but couldn't ever see.

Savagely, passionately, men shouted against the persecutors, denouncing them as lower than beasts. All during the time of torture they raged against their tormentors, kicking the cell doors until the screams of the afflicted man were lost in the drumming sound.

Perhaps that was why they did it.

And sometimes it was a woman, not a man, who screamed against those tormentors.

Babbling, saying these things in a jumble of words and sentences that only with difficulty could be built into sense,

Suleiman fought against the man who held him, and woke the others so that they sat up, shivering in the cold night air, aghast at the agony of that tortured man in their midst.

Tex held him down, calling: 'You're all right, brother. You're safe enough now . . .'

And then Suleiman began to tell of that day when the heavy, tramping footsteps halted outside his own cell door. It opened; a yellow light gleamed. He was standing there, sweating with fear, for this was the first time he had ever been in the secret police hands.

Tex sat in horror, sharing that moment with the man in his arms. Feeling the helplessness of it, of the evil that came in through that door.

Big men. Men in uniforms that were of good cloth and not like the second-hand British Army uniforms that the street police wore. Men who filled their uniforms, because they saw that they, at least, ate well.

Men with hard, yellow faces in that lamplight, and eyes that regarded him with . . . pleasure.

Suleiman went mad then, living again

that night. Living again through the torment of what was done to him, below the surface of the earth in that secret prison within the ancient Citadel. Tex, listening, felt the sweat pour from his own face, felt his mouth go dry with horror.

What they had done to their helpless prisoner would be written on the man's face and body whilever he lived. Now Tex understood — understood why a man should carry a face so brutally misshapen that even Nature would disclaim responsibility.

The others were awake and listening. Tex looked round. His two legionnaire comrades wouldn't understand, because they couldn't speak Arabic . . . Nicky Shaw, who was a smart newspaperwoman, wouldn't understand this gabble, either. But 'brahim, who was the son of a sheik, would understand, and Mahfra, too.

Then he saw their prisoner, Captain Sturmer of the Foreign Legion . . . Sturmer who had been a Nazi general in the North African fighting. Sturmer, who was wanted by the Allied War Crimes

Commission for atrocities.

Sturmer was sitting up as well as his bonds would allow. He was watching Suleiman, his head shoved forward as if intent, not wanting to miss a thing. And even in that near-darkness that a small moon did little to dissipate, it seemed to Tex that on Sturmer's face was no pity. Just — contempt.

Tex wanted to walk across and wipe that look off the Nazi's face. Instead he shook Suleiman the Hideous gently, and said, over and over again: 'Now, fellar, that's all over now. There ain't no one here to hurt you.'

'They went mad, in those cells about me.' Suleiman was almost rational as he described the horror of that scene in his delirium. 'Shouting, banging. Telling me not to give in, not to say anything.'

Suleiman the Hideous wept in his fever, out there under the cool night sky in the midst of the vast Sahara desert. For there was nothing he could have said to his tormentors, anyway. He knew nothing to tell them, only they wouldn't believe him. And that made the agony so much the worse — being tortured, because the secret police had made a mistake.

Now it was different, of course. Now he knew so many secrets that he couldn't ever let himself fall into those evil hands again.

In time he was quiet, and then everyone lay down to sleep. Tex, lowering the troubled man on to the soft desert sand, heard 'brahim, the sheik's son, say caustically: 'All was as I said. This dog is troublesome. All beggars are troublesome. He should have been left to die, and then we would have had the sleep we need.'

Tex nearly went across at that, but restrained himself. He knew Arabs, knew their philosophy. In 'brahim's world there were always dogs, and dogs could be tormented according to the will of those ordained by Allah to rule. Allah chose the leaders; it was for men to accept the wisdom of Allah, otherwise they must suffer.

'brahim had been born into the richly-caparisoned tent of a sheik, and his views were moulded accordingly. Tex shrugged and stretched himself to sleep.

His last impression was of Mahfra — Rain-in-Early-Summer — who was staring again at the sleeping, huddled form that was Suleiman the Hideous, her face a mask of fear and horror.

Tex's sleep was troubled, for he knew that much was to come in consequence of finding Suleiman the Hideous helpless in the desert. Perhaps the dream came to him that they should have killed Suleiman, but if it did he remembered it imperfectly when he awoke next morning.

Suleiman was trying to escape when Tex wakened with the first light of dawn. He was weak from the privations of the past few days, yet his will had brought him to his feet and sent him reeling across to the horses. Tex, who slept like a cat, heard the shuffle of bare feet across the sand, and leapt after him. Suleiman had his hand on the bridle of a horse. Their water was mostly on this beast, which was why Suleiman had chosen it.

Tex strode over, lean and forbidding in that half-light. Suleiman felt the hand on his shoulder and turned. He was a big man himself — nearly as tall as ex-Legionnaire Texas — and his face was close to Tex's. Tex saw the wreckage that had once been a man's face, saw those brown eyes looking calmly from it as if unafraid even if death followed instantly.

Tex looked at the horse, at the water bags on the saddle, and his voice was harsh. 'This is a fine way to repay us, fellar! You'd have us die of thirst in the desert, would you?'

That incongruous voice with its Scottish accent merely said, indifferently: 'Perhaps.' Suleiman shrugged. 'But it was not to be.'

He was swaying from weakness. Tex took him by the shoulder and pulled him away from the horse and made him sit down. He thought: 'The others don't know.' They were sleeping. He felt ashamed in some way, because he wanted to keep secret from them what this desert wanderer had proposed to do — as if he felt responsible for the man's actions because he, the leader of the party, had ordered mercy to be shown to him.

Then a movement caught his eye. The

glint of rising light upon glasses.

Ex-Nazi General Sturmer was awake and watching them.

Suleiman the Hideous stumbled and then sat down in the sand. Tex stood over him, his brow furrowed. Suleiman looked up, calmly, as if awaiting a verdict.

Tex asked, surprisingly: 'Where did you get that Scotch accent? And who are the Brotherhood of Tormented Men?'

The latter question seemed to shock Suleiman. Tex saw brown eyes dilate in horror saw real terror sweep across that monstrously ugly face. Then Suleiman tried to rise, but Tex pushed him back into the sand.

So Suleiman asked: 'What do you know of the Brotherhood?'

Tex shrugged. 'You were speaking in your dreams last night. You spoke much of them, friend.'

Suleiman let his eyes drop slowly. He was wondering how much his unguarded tongue had revealed. And he was thinking, with regret: 'He must die — all must die. They know too much.'

Tex recognised in that silence a

decision to say nothing about the intriguing Brotherhood, so he reverted to his first question. 'Your accent — ?'

Suleiman lifted his eyes, then. He was a man who could find mild humour in the most unexpected things. Now he said: 'Once I was of good family. I was a student at Edinburgh University. I shared lodgings with Ian McAllister, Rob Murray and wee Jamie Elliott. So my English has a Highland note to it.'

Tex nodded. It was a simple explanation. Then he said: 'Will you be able to take the trail today?'

'The trail?'

'Ride with us?'

Suleiman looked startled. He hadn't expected this. He'd been about to repay kindness by leaving them without most of their precious water supply; now all that this big American said was: 'Can you ride with us?'

Suleiman nodded, dragging himself to his feet again. He was a big, ragged figure, with the tatters of his galabier flapping in the morning breeze that always stirs across the sands with the first warming rays of the new-risen sun. He said, simply: 'I'm strong again. I have to be — have to go on.' Then his big brown eyes looked straight at Tex's and he said: 'You I don't understand. Other men would have killed me for what I was about to do.'

Tex made a bitter gesture with his hands. 'Killin'?' He said nothing more but went across to waken his friends.

They drank sparingly and ate of some dates and coarse brown bread that was in one of the saddlebags. With light had come the old apprehension, they were staring around the desert, uneasy and suspicious, as if expecting sudden assault by deadly enemies.

The battered pug face of one of the legionnaires lifted from an empty water skin. 'We ain't got much water now, Tex,' he griped. He had the clipped, unmusical accent of that village in New York City that calls itself Brooklyn. 'We got two-t'ree days' ride to the next waterhole, an' we ain't got more'n a day's water ration.'

They all turned and looked at Suleiman. 'brahim the sheik's son lifted his hands in

a gesture to heaven. 'It was as I said . . . '
He looked aloofly down his long, handsome nose at the scarecrow in their midst.
Only Tex was noticing the strength that
lay under those shapeless rags.

Tex grew a little impatient. It was all
right understanding the patrician Arab's
point of view, but, the hell, it was time
'brahim understood a Texan's viewpoint.

'Look, fellar,' he growled, 'don't get me
mad. We don't leave fellars — not even
beggars like Abdul here — to die of thirst
when we've got water.'

Nicky said, emphatically: 'No, sir, we
don't. And I'm going to stop liking you if
you keep on this theme. After all,' she
went on in rising indignation, 'isn't that
what we did for you — risked our lives to
save you?'

Imperturbably 'brahim the sheik's son
gave them the answer. It set them dancing
mad. 'But I am of noble blood, in lineal
descent of the Prophet himself. While this
— he is a *fella*.'

Tex just turned and said: 'Goddamn,
he's gettin' in my hair, this sheik.'

He stalked across to his horse. He knew

he had jeopardised the safety of his comrades by insisting on giving the stranger all the water he needed, but he also knew that he'd had no alternative — he wasn't made to pass a man by whose life depended on charity, no matter how it affected him.

Reaching his mount, he said, savagely: 'Okay, let's get movin'. Maybe this waterhole 'brahim talks about isn't as far as he thinks.'

Suleiman swayed uncertainly across towards the legionnaire. 'Man,' came that fantastic Scottish accent, 'there's no need to worry about water.' His hand waved to where hills showed clearly to the north of them, starkly revealed by the fresh bright sunshine of the morning. 'Little more than a day away is water good enough for any man, and in quantity sufficient for an army.'

That brought them all crowding round. Tex said: 'You know where it is?'

Suleiman nodded, his brown eyes intent on that lean Texan's face. 'That was my destination, until my water ran out.'

So Tex nodded. 'It's a bit out of our way, but — lead on, MacDuff.'

Then he did something that the quick-eyed Suleiman remembered. He looked searchingly west of them to where mighty mountains reached into the dazzling blue sky, before mounting his horse. Suleiman framed a question to ask later.

Instead he kept silent, and prepared to lead them to their death.

3

The Small Book

There was a bother about who should double up with the ragged beggar. Tex settled it. He hauled Suleiman the Hideous up behind him.

Suleiman had a curious effect on the Texan. Somehow he no longer saw the man as a beggar in soiled and tattered robes; instead he saw a man with an unusual mind, with a personality that came through those scars and sores on his face. He saw a man; and he was a man himself.

At noon they rested for a few hours, because the sun was too hot for them to travel. The ground had changed during their morning's journey: no longer was it loose sand, but now it was grey dirt, which supported an occasional clump of coarse grass and knee-high thorn bush. They were steadily climbing, too, along a mighty, sloping shelf that reached in to the foot of those bare, rocky hills ahead of them.

They sheltered from the intolerable heat in the shadow cast by a pile of fantastically eroded rocks that for no reason at all were jumbled together on that great plain. Suleiman had seemed relieved when they sighted the rocks, like a man who has been not too sure of the way he was going.

'Och, I thought I'd forgotten the way,' the Scots-speaking Arab said in relief as they swung down from their mounts. He seemed to have recovered most of his strength during that morning's ride, unlike the others who had been fatigued by it. But then Tex recognized his kind — strengthened by hardship, and surviving where others died.

A tough man, this Suleiman the Hideous, Tex kept thinking. Yet he had a feeling of confidence in the man; illogically he felt that under the awful mask of a face was a fine spirit.

He said, watching the easy way in which his saddle companion got down:

'Sully, don't you get no more ideas into your head about skedaddlin' with a hoss, savvy?'

He was anxious; he had a feeling he didn't want to be let down. So he looked at Suleiman and was relieved to see that big, shaven, turnip head with its ugly knitted skull cap nod. 'I'll no dae it again.'

Tex was satisfied. Suleiman watched that big, rangy Westerner as he walked away. He was thinking:

'There's no need for me to try to escape. They're coming with me . . . '

And it was essential that they did go with him, now that he knew his tongue had spoken when it should have remained locked in silence.

He trailed after Tex, thinking: 'How much did I say? How much do they know?' But without answers to those two important questions, he still knew they knew too much.

These Franks and this sheik had heard of the Brotherhood of Tormented Men. The Brethren were not yet ready for the world to know of them. So, there could be but one end to these compassionate strangers who had succoured him in the desert.

He regretted it, for he had a fine spirit. But what else was there to do?

The others drew away when that face of evil came into their midst. Suleiman saw it, remembered, and walked a distance apart. Then, imperturbably, he went to sleep for a few precious hours. Soon he would need his strength.

Lovely blonde Nicky Shaw crabbed across the sand and snuggled close against the Texan. The other two legionnaires watched with envy. They were comrades — friends — but Nicky Shaw was all that any man could desire — even in this arid waste.

Tex's face relaxed into a smile as he looked down at her. That tendril of blonde hair was getting in the way again. He wanted to push it back into place, but decided the energy required was too much for him in this baking heat. She looked better today, though; getting used to the hardships of desert-riding, he thought.

He found her blue eyes troubled, disconcerting.

'Tex,' she whispered, 'that man — '

'Suleiman?'

'He frightens me.'

Restlessly, for some reason feeling he had to defend the desert wanderer, Tex said: 'He cain't help his face, Nicky. Neither can Joe, there. Joe's no picture, but he don't scare you none.'

But Nicky shook her blonde head, still worrying. 'Tex, I've got a feeling about him. He's — he's so deep. All the time he's got thoughts that he won't let us see. Like now.'

Tex said, slowly; 'I know what you mean.' His eyes went across to the sleeping Suleiman. 'He looks like a beggar, but he's got the mind of a — ' He thought for a while. 'The mind of a scientist. I've never met an Arab like him. Not in the desert, anyway.'

Nicky clutched his hand. Tex was startled, realising how worried the girl was. 'Tex, I've got a feeling about him.'

'Such as?' He tried not to show how disturbed he was.

' . . . fear. I'm frightened. Scared to death of that — that face,' Nicky gulped. 'And yet, Tex, believe me I don't think that it's that hideous face that I'm frightened of; it's something underneath.'

Tex grumbled — grumbled to hide this uneasiness that the girl fostered within him. 'Aw, heck, Nicky, your words don't add up.'

Nicky pulled herself away, her face curiously fierce. 'They don't . . . I can't explain myself.' Her hands clutched together and jerked as if in ineffectual protest at her inability to make herself understood. 'But.. Tex . . . He's planning something, and we don't come out well in his plans.'

Tex stood up, his manner dogged. 'Goddamnit, Nicky, you scare a fellar,' he protested. 'Look, there's somethin' about Suleiman, something I like.'

She faced him; flashed — 'Or is it pity, you big boob? You look so big and tough and we all know you're as tender-hearted as the most sentimental old grand-mother.' Her voice broke. She came up to him and rubbed the sleeve of his faded old tunic. It was a gesture of the utmost affection. She loved big Hank Davidson, who had joined the French Foreign

Legion as Legionnaire Hank Texas, because he was so fine and kind and compassionate, so ready to defend the weak against the strong. And they all knew it and worshipped him for this trait — 'brahim, Mahfra, Joe Ellighan, and Rube who had held the soubriquet of 'The Schemer' back at Sidi-bel-Illah.

All followed him with a blind devotion — excepting ex-Nazi Sturmer, their prisoner, of course. Sturmer only wanted to cut Tex's head off.

'Pity?' Tex felt silly, because he didn't want to be like anybody's grandmarm.

'Yes.' Again she rubbed his sleeve. 'You're wanting to make up to him for that awful face men have given him. You're sorry for what he has had to suffer, and this is your way of showing it.'

He said: 'You're the screwiest of dames, Nicky. You talk like this much longer and there won't ever be a cast-out Noo York noospaper woman comin' lookin' for a job as housekeeper on the Davidson ranch.'

But he knew she was right.

It seemed an intolerably long time, waiting for the sun to decline sufficiently for them to be able to continue their journey. They lay on the hot sand and panted, the sweat coursing down their grey-powdered faces; their shirts made black patches where they stuck to their backs, and sweat soaked up through their boots and evaporated and left a rime of white salt crystal in the leather folds.

But in the end they came through. In time the worst heat was over and they were able to rise, ready to resume their journey.

They drank most of their water. It was warm, flat and seemed to have lost the property of slaking their thirst, but they knew it gave life to them and only wished they had more. Reluctantly they left in the waterskins sufficient only to carry them through the night.

As they were mounting, 'brahim, who seemed to have been worrying, strode up behind Tex and said: 'By the Beard of the Prophet, there is no water this way.'

Tex stiffened, his unease crystallising. He turned and looked into that handsome Arab's face. 'brahim's eyes were big and hot and angry.

'I swear there is trickery,' 'brahim said, exaggerating his emotions as all young Arabs do. 'I know this country well, having hunted gazelles many times in these mountains, and I say there is no waterhole this way.'

Tex looked over his saddle towards the hills. They were unlovely and sinister in shape; there was only bare rock, purple-brown from this distance, squeezed up from the desert in the final agonies of a shrinking, cooling world.

Not all purple-brown, however. There was a patch of whiteness ahead, like a smear against the mountain side. That patch had been growing larger and whiter all morning, and vaguely Tex had speculated about it.

Tex said, tiredly: 'Mebbe you don't know this country like Suleiman does. Mebbe there is a waterhole.' He grappled with the problem for a moment and then posed their plight in question form. 'What's the answer, anyway? We're out of water; you don't know of water anywhere around here, an' Sully says he does. So . . . mebbe we'd better take a chance on Sully, huh?'

'brahim showed his anger. 'Suleiman the Hideous is of the gutters of Cairo. He is not to be trusted. He is a political criminal and such men deserve one treatment.' He pulled a lean, brown finger across his throat.

Suleiman was listening. As if feeling that presence Tex and 'brahim simultaneously turned. They saw that tall big-boned scarecrow in his rags, saw that monstrous face under the knitted skull cap. Suleiman said nothing but patiently waited to get up behind Tex again.

Tex growled: 'We go where Sully takes us,' and 'brahim stamped away in annoyance at that. Tex swung into the saddle and gave Suleiman a lift up. Then they started to ride north again.

As he watched that growing patch of whiteness, Tex let his mind turn over from one subject to another. Mostly about Suleiman, the Arab who had been educated at Edinburgh University. He thought: Sully knows where there is water. He's not taken us into the desert to let us all die just for the fun of it. No man committed suicide that way.

After a while he looked again at those looming hills, and his unease grew. For they were heading back across the Tripolitanian border, were riding into French territory again. And that meant they were running the risk of meeting French troops — perhaps the Foreign Legion — and they were *poumpists*, deserters who might lose their lives if they were captured.

He shrugged, trying to dismiss the thought. Water dominated desert strategy always, now as in the warfare of the early '40s. Water — or lack of, it — dictated this detour north, and they simply had no alternative.

His fingers sought the bolt of his Lebel rifle, easing it a little to reassure himself that in emergency it would not be sanded up. The whiteness ahead was growing larger.

Just before sundown, even before they had halted for their evening rest, 'brahim lost his temper and came spurring up to the double-laden horse that led the cavalcade.

His eyes glared at Suleiman, sitting

behind the big Texan. 'Dog,' he thundered, 'this way there is no water. What trickery are you up to, O Man of Evil Face?'

Tex reined and shouted: 'Shut up, blast you!' 'brahim was a friend, a good comrade, but he was trying on the nerves. To the Texan's democratic view on life, these insults to an afflicted man were unpardonable. Nicky came up, but 'brahim had spoken in Arabic, so she didn't know what it was about.

Then Suleiman replied. Tex didn't understand the ragged scarecrow easily, because the language of the Nile differs considerably from the Arabic of other parts of the continent, yet he finally understood.

Suleiman said: 'O Son of a Sheik, this way truly we will find water; Few know of it, but I am one who does.'

Then Tex realised that this was not the crude patois of the Nile gutters, but the Arabic of a cultured, educated man. Of course, he should have expected it, in a man who had been wealthy enough to go to Edinburgh to study, but Suleiman's appearance didn't fit with such things, and consequently this new revelation came as a surprise to the observant Texan.

But 'brahim didn't notice it. 'brahim was bad-tempered and arrogant. In futile fury he replied with sarcasm. 'Only the Brotherhood of Tormented Men know of this place. Is that it, O Thing Unclean?'

Suleiman's eyes seemed to fix on that arrogant, bad-tempered young face, so recently bereft of its beard. For a long moment they held the young sheik, and finally it was 'brahim who withdrew his gaze. And 'brahim had seen murder in Suleiman's soul; 'brahim knew then what was in the tormented man's mind.

Tex got down, grumbling. 'We might as well take our rest now,' he declared. He hated quarrelling; was upset because he could feel these vague undercurrents of feelings of violence and yet could do nothing about them.

'We'll go on during the night.' According to Suleiman, another three or four hours would bring them to water.

'brahim came back at that. Mahfra, the

peasant girl who had once helped the party and was now travelling with them to this marvellous America she had heard about — Mahfra was standing by 'brahim's side, her fascinated eyes on that ugly, pain-formed face of Suleiman the Hideous. It was as if she couldn't tear her gaze away.

'brahim said urgently: 'No. Do not let us approach those hills during darkness.' He wheeled on the silent Suleiman. 'I fear treachery. I want daylight, so that I can see it and face it.'

Suleiman lifted his hands, palm upwards. 'As you will, O Sheik 'brahim. We have water enough for a start tomorrow.' He lowered himself to the ground, his big-boned ankles and massive feet showing for an instant under his long, tattered *galabier*.

Tex looked at the girl and saw their tiredness. A night's sleep in the coolness that only darkness could bring would do them a lot of good. They would go on with the early light of day.

They drank and ate as much as their little appetites demanded. Then they stretched themselves on the sand and waited for the last rays of the nearly-obscured sun to ebb.

For a while there was quietness. Then Nicky rolled towards Tex, stretched with his kepi over his face. He heard her whisper: 'I fear this Suleiman, Tex, yet — oh, I am so sorry for him.'

He shoved back his hat. These blue eyes of the American girl were on the nearby form of Suleiman, and they were troubled and filled with compassion at the same time.

She said: 'That face . . . it puts him apart from other men — us. But was it his fault? It — it seems so hard that he should sit alone, seems wrong we should shun him.'

Tex stroked the arm that was no longer quite so rounded but still soft and shapely. She was a fine girl, this newspaperwoman from New York; she thought the way he did.

He asked: 'Wal, why don't you go'n talk with him?' But he knew the answer.

There was pain in her eyes. 'I can't — can't bear to look at him. I feel I must stare and show my horror, and I — I don't want to hurt him any more. He's been hurt enough.'

Tex's eyes flickered towards Mahfra. She was watching the long, silent form of Suleiman, stretched twenty yards away from the party. He saw the back of that dark, glossy head only, but could picture the expression on her face. It was as if she couldn't keep her eyes off that man so well-named the Hideous.

He thought: 'The sooner we get Mahfra away from this fellar the better.'

It couldn't be good for a girl to maintain such a morbid interest in the man with the tortured face, and there was no knowing the tides of resentment that might be in him because of her wide-eyed horror. Yes, better get Suleiman away from the party pronto.

Nicky said: 'He doesn't affect you like he affects we others, Tex.'

Tex rolled on his side and began to tuck away that rebellious strand of blonde hair. His fingers were clumsy yet gentle.

'Mebbe I don't see men the way others do. I reckon I see past his ugly pan and into his soul. After all, it's a man's personality that shines through — that's the man, not his face.'

She understood, though he was not able to explain easily. She asked: 'What kind of a man is he really, underneath?'

He said again: 'Something fine. He's just the opposite of what he looks.' His eyes stared into the gathering darkness that was so welcome but could hide so many enemies. 'I figger Sully's quite a man.'

'You think 'brahim's wrong? Sully won't do us any harm?'

'Sully's grateful to us for saving his life. Sully won't do us wrong.'

Sully turned over at that and they saw his twisted, distorted features, felt, rather than saw, that his eyes were resting broodingly upon them. They were not to know that Suleiman the Hideous found his thoughts distasteful. For he was a fine man, and he would have preferred to have rewarded these people rather than plan their death.

Nicky turned away, her eyes sick. She could feel what this man must have

49

suffered to have been moulded into this form. She whispered: 'Go to him, Tex. Speak with him as a friend. He will be grateful I'm sure.'

Tex sighed, then climbed slowly on to his feet. In half an hour there would be complete darkness — then merciful rest for the next twelve hours. He walked over to the reclining Arab, followed by the eyes of all his party. 'brahim's were angry and resentful. He had grown bitterly antagonistic towards the desert wanderer whom they had succoured.

Tex looked down. Suleiman regarded him with passive brown eyes that disguised any thoughts in his mind. The Westerner lowered himself alongside the scarecrow.

Suleiman was shrewd. He came up on his elbow and said, softly; prolonging his r's in that fascinating Scots accent: 'You have taken pity on my loneliness? Aye?'

'It was Nicky.' He gestured behind him. 'The American girl, you know. She figgered you were kinda lonely.'

Suleiman nodded. Spoke calmly: 'I am always the loneliest of men. My face acts as a barrier. But sometimes I am in a company — which has its own afflictions, and then we notice them not.'

Tex nodded. He knew that Suleiman was talking about the Brotherhood. He was beginning to get ideas about the Tormented Men.

Suleiman said, softly: 'But it was a good thought. I am grateful to the lady.' He shrugged. 'It is a pity,' he said, but didn't explain what was the pity.

Brown Semitic eyes met grey, Nordic ones. Suleiman said: 'My face doesn't worry you, brother.'

'I don't seem to see it as the others do.'

'You are a remarkable man, Legionnaire Texas.'

'Ex-legionnaire,' corrected Tex with a tight smile.

'Still a remarkable man.' Suleiman sat up. He was thinking. His thoughts ran: 'Why not? The information won't do him any good. Soon he will be dead.'

Meanwhile, why not be friendly, why not discourse on interesting topics?

'I have not always been like this. There was a time when I was much as other men.' That warped face split into the semblance of a grin. It was frightening, ghastly — yet Tex could feel a warmth to it, as of humour.

'Never much to look at, mind you. My father was a Syrian, my mother a Copt from the Upper Nile. You know the people of the higher waters?' Tex shrugged. He'd met them but that didn't mean to say he had studied them to any extent.

'There's dark colour in their veins. When I was born I arrived with a big, turnip head, broad cheekbones and massive features.' That grin again. 'I was no beauty, but I was an oil-painting compared with how I look now.'

He was fumbling under his rags. Suddenly his hand brought out a small, hard-backed book. He grinned and said: 'This would cost me my life if it were found on me by certain people.'

'The political police?'

'Of many countries.'

Suleiman flipped open the little book. Tex saw names and descriptions, photographs, some full face, some profile, as the pages riffled open. Then Suleiman let him read what was printed on the first blue page within the book. It said:

SECRET
Service de la Sureté Publique, Caire

Suleiman said: 'This is the secret list of men and women wanted for political offences by the Egyptian Government.'

'Your picture is there?'

'Before they . . . worked on my face.'

Suleiman opened it at a page. Tex stared at the photograph of a stranger. He saw a young man, full of vigour and personality; a man with deep colour in his veins — big-headed, massive-featured. Not good-looking, as Suleiman had said, but not repulsive as he was now.

All Tex could say was: 'The years have changed you.'

'The years,' added Suleiman dryly, ' — and men.'

Out of curiosity Tex took the book. Under Suleiman's picture he read: 'Extudiant a Edinburgh.' He looked at other pictures, saw others who had been to the same university. Mostly young men, tarboshed, moustached, cold-eyed as is the way when men face a camera in the hands of a policeman.

He read one description: 'Ahmed Ramadan Zayan, Alexandrie. Dangereux. Suspecté de meutre politique . . . '

Suspected of political murder . . .

'Nice fellars,' Tex said. Suleiman's picture was in this gallery. Suspected of political murders . . .

'Some.' Suleiman shrugged indifferently. 'Not all.'

'The best,' said Tex ironically, 'being the ones that have been to Edinburgh University.' Curiosity bit him. 'How come so many students of Edinburgh get unpopular with the secret police of Egypt?'

Again that indifferent shrug. 'Perhaps we who go there see a democracy as fine as any on earth. At first we marvel at it, at the dignity of Scotsmen, their freedom and sense of equality with other men. When we go home to Egypt we cannot forget what we have seen, and we get into trouble because we find ourselves fighting against the oppression of tyrant kings and selfish pashas. In that book,' ended Suleiman, 'you will find the names of forty-four former students at Edinburgh University.'

Tex handed back the interesting little book. 'How come you got it?'

'There was a secret service agent who liked pickles. It gave him a thirst, and there was only cognac to slake it. When he was dead drunk I went through his pockets and took the book. He never knew who had paid for those pickles and that bottle of raw cognac, though he'd been carrying my picture in his pocket for months.'

Tex said: 'You're quite a man.' He understood about that surprising Scottish accent, and now he wanted to ask: 'Who are the Brotherhood of Tormented Men? What are they doing?' But he didn't. He had a feeling that that was one question this big, ugly Arab would not answer.

Suleiman talked, because he liked this drawling-voiced man from a Western democracy. He talked because he knew no harm could come from his talking, because this Westerner wouldn't be alive within twenty-four hours.

He talked because he knew Sheik 'brahim was watching them suspiciously, sullen-faced and raging at him as being the cause of his present discomfiture. He wanted to go on annoying 'brahim, because after all this son of a sheik was the enemy they were fighting against.

They? The Brotherhood, of course . . . that Brotherhood of the damned and the lost whose existence must not be spoken of outside the circle.

'I had a wealthy father. I went to Scotland, and my eyes were opened to how unnecessary was the suffering in my own land. When I returned I found I had to speak against the oppression and tyranny.'

'You became a reformer?'

'Unskilled but enthusiastic,' Suleiman nodded.

'An' then the police got to tailin' you.'

'Yes. I was followed — hounded — finally caught. They tortured me. They thought I was a member of some political organisation, and they wanted me to betray my comrades.'

Tex said, gently: 'You don't need to go on with that part of your story, fellar. You told enough in your delirium last night.'

Suleiman bowed his big head meekly, thankfully. He was grateful to this big Texan for his consideration. This Westerner was a fine man. It was unfortunate that he would have to go . . .

'They shouted, 'You are bolchévique.' But I wasn't, and in time they believed me. Then they called me Khédiviste, extrémiste, assassin, anarchiste. For each I was tortured, until they were sure my denials were the truth. That is why I suffered so much — because I knew nothing and could tell them nothing, but they took a long time to believe me. Then they threw me out.'

'And then?'

'Outside was a Tormented Man to see me, to speak with me, and to tell me what I must do.' Suleiman's eyes were in shadow, and his thoughts were far away to that moment that had begun a fiercely new but dangerous life for him.

He didn't speak of his work in many

capitals with the Brotherhood. Instead he turned the conversation. 'You know so much of me — what about you?'

He looked significantly across at the silent, malignant prisoner who had once been an arrogant Nazi general.

Tex said: 'He's the most evil man in the world, that fellar. Too bad to be killed out of hand, I reckon. He's wanted for war crimes — went an' hid in the Foreign Legion. We caught him — now we're tryin' to make the coast so as to take him to stand trial for the killin' of a thousand Americans.'

He didn't add that one of those Americans was his brother, Major John Davidson.

With that he rose and went back to where Nicky Shaw lay; for it was now nearly dark and he knew she would want him by her side. He was a man who gave courage to others, this big, brave Texan.

He left Suleiman to lie awake and look at the stars and think of the life he had led since those cool, formative years in Scotland. A man without rest; a man hunted wherever he went.

They had tracked him from Egypt when the call came for the Brotherhood to strike. They'd followed him to the Delta, to Alexandria — to the crowded waterfront with its motley assortment of shipping, and seamen from fifty different countries.

From the moment he had set off, he had known that his life wasn't worth a candle if he fell into those secret agents' hands again. They were hunting with the intention of killing him on sight.

But he had eluded them, had smuggled himself into a Greek *caique* that was sailing up to Tripoli . . . and they'd been waiting for him, when he came ashore.

The relentless hunt had driven him into the desert before he was properly equipped. In consequence he had nearly died, and only the luck of meeting these infidels had saved his life.

He turned over. He was thinking that for the success of his plans he mustn't be the first to enter the Valley-where-men-go-blind. The Brethren must be there before him.

In the night they all wakened. Tex felt

Nicky reach out and clutch him in the darkness. He whispered a fierce, 'Keep quiet!' to his stirring companions, and then was quiet himself.

There was no moon, only stars to light the world, and that they did ineffectually. A night wind stirred and moaned over the desert.

They heard movement, not too far away, the regular shush-shush of feet treading on loose, dry sandy soil. A big body of men was passing. Tex couldn't tell if they were afoot or on horseback. He didn't go across to find out — whoever they were, they couldn't be friends, he knew.

The noise gradually faded. The danger was passing.

Then one of their horses began to whinny a greeting to the passers-by.

4

Water

Tex seemed to fling himself straight from the ground across to that dim shape that was a horse. He clutched it round the soft nose and pinched its nostrils to keep it quiet. The horse ploughed around for a few seconds, then became passive as it recognised his body smell.

Tensely they waited, listening. But nothing happened. The distant murmur of movement dropped away altogether. Tex released his hold on the horse and came back to his companions. Nicky was trembling, he knew, so he put his arm round her to comfort her.

She said: 'Thank heaven they didn't hear that wretched horse, whoever they were.'

Tex didn't say anything. He knew they must have heard it. A whinnying horse can be heard for five miles in a desert, and those people had crossed within a quarter of a mile of them. For their own reasons they had ignored the sound.

He couldn't understand it, but he took no chances. He told his comrade legionnaires to stay awake and keep watch, and all night the three crouched, Lebels ready, looking into the darkness and preparing to shoot at the slightest suspicious movement.

But dawn came without disturbance, and with the first faint gleams of light they prepared to move. Better to get on their way before the heat came that stifled energy and crippled movement.

They emptied their water skins. They had little enough and their throats craved more. Brooklyn Joe Ellighan looked at the flattened goatskin and said: 'I figger we just gotta find water now. Ain't nuttin' else for it.' He looked at Suleiman the Hideous and said: 'You'd better be right, brudder, 'bout that waterhole.'

Suleiman climbed up behind Tex. 'Soon,' he assured them, 'you will be able to bathe in it.'

The prisoner was tied to a mount,

Rube Koskowsci sitting behind, then the party moved off. For a while it was easy going, almost cool because of the absence of direct sunlight upon them. During that time they talked, Tex and the scarecrow clinging behind him.

They talked about many things, for they were men who had travelled and seen the world. It was just when the sun had cleared the eastern sand dunes, and the sudden heat left them gasping, that they began to speak of desire.

'You're up here for something,' Tex said, looking round over his shoulder at the Arab. 'Here.' He waved his hand round impatiently. 'What'n hell's name does anyone want to come out here for? What's brought you here, Suleiman?' — the first direct question on the subject.

'Desire.' Suleiman's brooding eyes were ahead, narrowed against a glare too strong even for his accustomed vision. 'I want to rid the world of men who create torment for others.' Then he shut up like a clam.

Tex shook his head admiringly, incredulously. 'You sure are some Ay-rab,' he said. 'Ain't there anythin' else you desire?'

'Yes.' Suleiman withdrew his eyes from the distance. 'One other thing I desire.' He looked at Tex, straight into those level grey eyes, and then turned his gaze away. 'I'm a man, O Texan, with a man's desires. And I want what all men want, but my face is a barrier against it.'

'You want a woman?'

Suleiman shrugged. 'A girl — sweetheart — wife. Or a woman. Call it what you will. But there's the hunger in my heart, that's what I want.' And then he said, deliberately: 'That's what I'll get, soon.'

Tex's head jerked round. He followed Suleiman's eyes. They were on Mahfra's slim form, riding up with 'brahim, the sheik's son.

He said nothing to that, but his thoughts retained the subject for the next mile of plodding progress. He was disturbed and uneasy — and filled with compassion. Suleiman was a man and must have man's needs, yet that awful, mutilated face was against him. Mahfra had shown her naive horror sufficiently to give an answer to Suleiman's hopes in that direction.

What disturbed Tex was the complete certainty with which Suleiman had made his statement. Suleiman was determined ... that must mean trouble, especially trouble from 'brahim, who wanted lovely Mahfra for himself.

Tex lifted his head to look before them. The sweat was coursing down his cheeks now, and the dust from the desert came up in clouds and matted his face. Once he had hated it — hated that tingling powder up his nostrils, the weight of settling dust upon his eyelashes and eyebrows — but now he didn't seem to notice it. Now all he noticed was the intolerable heat of the near-tropical sun which seemed to press with real weight upon him. He never got used to that. In Texas it had never seemed so fierce, so malignant.

His eyes narrowed as a fierce white light bit into them. They had approached to within a few miles of that white patch on the hillside, and now it seemed to occupy the whole horizon before them.

The bright sunlight, reflecting on that glittering white mass, was blinding in intensity. Tex had to regard the place covertly, his eyes nearly closed, his head to one side. And he felt the heat of reflected light hot upon his cheek as he did so.

He saw that the hillside was clothed with a gleaming white substance, saw shadows and knew there were valleys within the stuff. So far as he could judge, the whiteness stretched for a good mile along the base of the range of hills, tapering to a point about a quarter of a mile up the rocky slope.

He reined in his horse. Instinct came to warn him of danger. Twisting in his saddle he looked at the man who sat behind him. Suleiman regarded him silently, his brown eyes devoid of expression.

Tex asked: 'You want us to go straight on towards that whiteness?' Suleiman nodded. Tex squinted back at the mountain slope. The others were closing around on their sweating, saliva-flecked horses. 'You reckon there's water there?'

Again Suleiman nodded.

'brahim, his mouth obscured by his burnouse, pushed his mount closer. When his neckcloth dropped, Tex saw the fierce anger on that face and grew ready for action immediately.

'brahim was too young to maintain the dignity that was traditional to his class. Now he shouted in Arabic: 'As God is my judge, there is no water before us!'

Tex's face was impassive, not showing his disturbed feelings beneath. 'Suleiman says there is.'

'Do I not know these parts better than any crawling beggar?' 'brahim was arrogant, contemptuous. 'Do not all men of my tribe know that hereabouts is no water of any kind? We have been misled by this camel dung whose life we so mistakenly saved.' His voice was a shout of passion now; 'brahim knew the terrors of death by thirst in this awful desert that had been home to him all his life.

'brahim had had enough of living in deserts, anyway, which was why he had thrown in his lot with Tex's party — and why he had shaved away a beard that had been his glory among his own people. 'brahim had decided to become an American, and apparently the land of Gillette did not nowadays run to hair on the chin.

Suleiman just said, simply: 'The camel dung is not mistaken, for the crawling beggar can lead us to water within the hour.'

Tex translated for the benefit of his comrades. The big, flat, battered pan of ex-Legionnaire Joe Ellighan cracked open to one side and a trickle of Brooklyn issued. 'What're we waitin' for? Let's go!'

'brahim shouted: 'No. We have gone far enough. This wretch is mad.' He even reached down and grabbed the rein of Tex's mount as if to restrain him. Tex was startled to see the real emotion on that long, thin, good-looking Arab's face. No doubt, 'brahim was really worked up; 'brahim was in a genuine panic at the thought of going forward.

Quickly he demanded: 'What's on your mind, brother? What's scarin' you 'bout that white stuff ahead?' Because he knew it was something to do with that glistening mass, so unusual in the desert.

'brahim tugged urgently at the faded blue tunic sleeve. 'That way, O Teksuss, is disaster for all of us, disaster that must end in death.' His molten brown eyes turned angrily, hatefully, upon the man who had brought them there. 'You know this place of evil. Tell them, then, by what name is this place known to the desert folk.'

Suleiman knew and told them. 'It is called, The Valley-where-men-go-blind.'

Tex remembered the biting glare reflecting from the whiteness and he demanded: 'Well, is it true? Do men go blind through lookin' at that damn' stuff?' 'brahim was nodding emphatically. Suleiman's silence gave the answer also. So Tex asked, almost querulously: 'Then what's it mean, Sully? What're we doin', headin' for that place?' Another mile and the glare would be intolerable.

Suleiman shrugged. 'I wanted to approach by night. We have no water to help us through the day and must go forward now.' He was very matter-of-fact about it, and it irritated Tex — it inflamed 'brahim, however.

'In his madness he would blind us first and then leave us to die within that white hell — to die of thirst.' His fist rose as if to strike down their guide from his seat behind Tex. It was his natural way of showing displeasure to one of the *fellahin* class. Tex hadn't time to intervene, but found it unnecessary, anyway.

He saw Suleiman's cropped head shove forward as if to invite the blow, saw those brown, curiously calm eyes looking straight into the young Arab's. It might have been that look, so unlike the usual cringing of the peasant or beggar Arab, that stopped the blow, or it might have been the closeness of that appallingly tortured face that could look so evil to most men. At any rate, it seemed that 'brahim faltered, and then his hand dropped, and the young Arab looked sullen and displeased with himself.

Tex heard a sharp exclamation from Mahfra, and didn't know whether the fear back of it was for 'brahim, who wanted her, or for Suleiman . . . who wanted her, too.

70

The horses milled in some confusion at the little disturbance, and bonny, blue-eyed Nicky came riding her mount between the men. Tex saw care and anxiety on that small, oval face that could look so fresh and Nordic in spite of the increasing tan. Nicky was keeping her head; she knew that fighting wasn't going to ease their problems. Rube and Elegant were shouting something, but Tex didn't know what they were saying.

He shouted them all down, getting the men apart. 'Goldarn it, keep your hands to yourself, all of you!' One glance at the other legionnaires' faces told him they were now siding with 'brahim. That face of Suleiman's was against him.

'You tell me about that stuff,' he ordered 'brahim, jerking his head towards the whiteness.

Sullenly 'brahim complied. 'All men who are of the desert know that to look full upon that hillside when the sun is high is to be instantly smitten with blindness. The glare is more than human eyes can stand.'

His eyes shot hatred at the silent,

impassive scarecrow in the tattered *galabier*.

'We are going towards the Valley-where-men-go-blind, yet I ask why? For is it not known that within that valley there is no water, nor can there be because of the substance that creates the whiteness.'

'And that is . . . ?'

'Salt.'

Tex looked again at that white coating to the sloping hillside. Salt. He had seen lakes of salt before, shimmering white and crystalline, but never a mountain of it, like this. He was appalled; for what water, fit for drinking, could there be within that mass of salt?

Suleiman stirred behind him. He caught the swirl of tattered robe as a bony leg cocked over the horse's hindquarters. Then Suleiman, hideous under that knitted skullcap that revealed rather than concealed the shorn ugliness of his head, looked up at them. Tex saw not the scarred and mutilated face, but only the calmness of the soul revealed through the man's eyes. Suleiman was an enigma to the Westerner, but he felt that he was beginning to understand him.

He heard that Scottish voice come from that Arab throat: 'There's water enough where I am taking you. What made that cascade of salt in the first place? Why, water, of course.' His eyes flickered towards the hostile 'brahim. 'brahim was holding a rifle in a way that Tex didn't like.

'For centuries a spring has bubbled from the mountainside, evaporating as it spilled over the hot, rocky surface, and leaving behind a deposit of salt that has grown in time to be a mountain. And that spring still flows, though few men dare brave the Valley-where-men-go-blind to find it.'

'If what you say is true, what good is salt water to us?' 'brahim's tone was fiercely angry. For did not all men know that much of the water to be found in the desert was salty, and wasn't it madness and death to drink of it?

'The water is salty — but not too salty,' said Suleiman calmly. He spoke like a teacher to a petulant child, so very sure of himself. His eyes lifted to Tex's. 'I will lead you to it; I will walk, holding the reins of your horse. The other horses will follow.'

'And the whiteness . . . the glare . . . the blindness?' asked Tex grimly.

They were all waiting for Suleiman's answer, grouped there under the Sahara sun on that grey scrub desert.

Suleiman said: 'My eyes are good; if I am careful I shall suffer no harm. But you — you of the Northern grey eyes — you must not look at all or you will be blinded for life. When we get nearer, all must bandage their eyes — '

'And leave us truly blind within your care?' 'brahim, suspicions strongly crystallised now.

'There is no alternative.' Suleiman shrugged.

They looked at each other. Tex knew that his companions were uncertain, troubled. Somehow he had confidence in the Arab, but he knew it wasn't shared by the others. Uneasily he wondered if they weren't more right in their judgment than their leader. 'brahim's roughly-expressed suspicions had also had their effect.

Curiously, it was the prisoner who settled the matter for them. They heard the thin, colourless clerk-like voice of the Nazi war leader, former-General Herman Sturmer, now a captain in the ranks of the French Foreign Legion.

'There is no alternative' they heard the man say. 'We must trust this Arab, and we die if our trust is misplaced.' And then he added, with the air of a man pronouncing judgment: 'It is as the man tells us, running water will not be saturated with salt, only that which is in lakes and is evaporating constantly under the heat of the sun.'

It was almost the first tune he had spoken since he had fallen into their hands. Now all looked at him

They saw that thin, almost weak-looking form and it seemed impossible to believe that he could be a man of such cold ferocity as they knew him. But they did know it, and weren't taken in by his rimless glasses that gave him a mildly clerical air.

They knew him to be a cold-blooded killer; for besides his war crimes, was he not head of the *partizans*, that body of headhunters, mostly renegade Arabs, who scoured the desert for deserters from the French Foreign Legion? And had they not seen him, quite dispassionately, loose his savage followers on to a deserter and secure his head within minutes?

. . . and weren't they, in fact, fleeing from just those dreaded *partizans* right at this moment?

Tex found himself repeating, mechanically: 'There is no alternative.'

With that Suleiman nodded, and it seemed there was satisfaction in that brief inclination of the head. He turned and began to walk towards the white cascade that sheeted the hillside before them. He retained his hold on the reins of Tex's horse, and the beast, with hanging head, had to follow. The other horses came into line behind the leader.

For half an hour they trudged, and now the sun was almost directly overhead, and the heat was like being in an inferno. It came reflecting off that white salt mass in waves of sickening warmth, and they rode stooped against it, as if this way they could shed it from their bodies. And they rode with eyes averted, because they found that even from this distance it hurt to look upon that white mountain.

Tex wondered at the Arab who led the way. Wondered that any man could find energy to walk in this heat . . . wondered that his eyes could be open sufficiently for him to see his way. Yet he walked unhesitatingly forward, as if sure of his ground.

After half an hour, Suleiman called back: 'Soon we enter the valley where men go blind. You had better cover your eyes, for if you are startled and open them against the white light you will surely lose your sight.'

Tex obediently began to fix a neckcloth round his eyes. His last vision was of his companions doing the same, only hesitantly, reluctantly . . . 'brahim was pulling his burnouse up over his nose, but wasn't bandaging his eyes.

'brahim was too suspicious, too sure there was a trap somewhere. And he wanted to see what was coming, when it came.

That was 'brahim's lookout, Tex thought, and then he tightened the bandage across his eyes.

He felt his mount go forward, as if the reins had been tugged by Suleiman. He knew the other horses would be following behind. Then he felt a hand on his sleeve — stiffened. And realised that Nicky had ridden alongside him. By the way her hand fumbled down towards his, he knew she was blindfolded, too.

He heard her clear young voice say: 'Funny, I get scared when I can't see you, you big lug.' Then she was holding his hand and showing by the pressure of her fingers how scared she was of their situation.

He said, as calmly as he could: 'We'll be all right. Sully won't let us down. I c'n almost hear that runnin' water already.'

There was silence. And then Nicky said, softly so that no one else would hear: 'Tex, I don't share your confidence. I think Suleiman's up to something — and we're going to lose out on the deal, whatever it is.'

And then she told him something else.

'I've been watching Sturmer. Oh, Tex, you should see the way he looks at Suleiman. He — he seems to find pleasure in looking at what they did to that man's face.' It seemed that she gulped back a horror at the thought, Then she told Tex: 'Sturmer is sure that Suleiman is betraying us. I can read that in his eyes. And he's banking somehow on turning the tables on us when Sully shows his hand.'

It wasn't a comforting thought. But Tex just sighed wearily and said: 'We've come so far and now there's no turnin' back, Nicky. It's certain death if we turn an' try to find water in this desert. Whereas it is less certain if we put our trust in Sully.'

Rather weakly he found himself adding: 'Aw, heck, Nicky, we saved his life, didn't we? You don't think anyone could be heel enough to do a double on us after that. Nope, I figger Sully's no heel, in spite of his face. I figger he'll lead us to that water, you see if he don't!'

Even Nicky tried to believe, too. 'After all,' he heard her sigh, 'if we don't find water, he dies too.'

By now they were gasping from the heat and the horses were suffering and making their protest. Though they couldn't see it, already the grey soil under them was beginning to whiten where the fine salt had been blown out from the main mass, and sparkling little crystals threw up heat at them, adding to the torture of the sun overhead.

Then, in time, they came right up to the salt mountain — and they knew from that moment the meaning of hell.

They didn't know it, but they had entered a narrow gorge that had been washed out of the deep salt by occasional storms in winter. Here there was no shadow, because the summer sun was directly overhead, and so the heat blazed down on to them and was reflected by the pure white walls on either side on to their drooping, helpless bodies.

They were climbing, too, and it must have been agony for their poor horses. Tex felt a scorching blast rise up from below that seemed to shrivel his skin. He knew he was drying up in the heat, knew they could only suffer this torment for a few minutes at the most and then they must go mad in an effort to escape the grilling.

He had been thirsty long before they reached this whiteness, but now, in that terrible bath of fire, he felt a raging thirst such as he had never considered possible before.

'How much longer? How much longer?' his thoughts panicked as the horses stumbled along. Nicky was holding his hand so hard that she was hurting. She must have been suffering the same, must have been terrified.

Then they heard Suleiman's voice ringing loudly between the confines of the white walls.

'Only another minute — and then there will be peace and rest for you.'

Peace and rest . . . for you. Tex found himself repeating the phrase, and he didn't like it. For you? Why not, 'For us?'

'We're walking into a trap!' his thoughts thundered. Now he knew it, just as the others had suspected long before. Now he was certain that Suleiman was planning to do them harm.

Yet, what could they have done before,

even if he had known this . . . ?

Astonishingly, just when the heat was hotter, more unendurable than before, their agony was over. All in one second they passed from out of the burning hell into a coolness that was almost cold.

And there was shadow, too, relief from that raging sun. They felt it even through their bandages. Coolness and a cessation from that awful glare . . .

Tex heard water running. His horse was hurrying forward now without need for guidance. Tex started to tear off his bandage, started to shout, exultantly: 'Sully did it! We're there — with water at last!'

And part of his joy was because he hadn't wanted to believe bad things about Suleiman; he'd wanted the man to prove his words and lead them to water and safety . . .

His eyes cleared of the bandage. They adjusted themselves. He saw white walls rearing together overhead, like the walls of some mighty cathedral. He saw the darkness of a broad, rocky floor. The light was almost dim, so that for a moment all detail was lost.

And then it seemed to him that the earth was yielding up arms and legs, bodies and faces. Men were rising, apparently from nowhere, were lurching towards his party as if spewed from the ground.

Before he could move, his Lebel was snatched from his hands.

5

Treachery

Suleiman was shouting, his words echoing in that cavern under the salt mountain. A horse whinnied with terror, and a girl screamed. And then clawing hands dragged him from his horse and hurled him to the ground.

They let go of him at that, as if satisfied that he was harmless. He rolled over, the rock floor cold beneath him, welcome even in that moment of peril after the heat of the Valley-where-men-go-blind.

He saw the horses go trotting eagerly away towards a depression in the rock floor. Saw them go up to their bellies in water that broke in waves against their dust-powdered hides. Then their muzzles were immersed and they were drinking as if they would never stop. Some men went running to pull them out.

Tex's attention was jerked back to the

men who stood around them.

Nicky and the others had been dragged off their horses, too — even Sturmer, who had been tied with his feet underneath his mount's belly. Now they were all together, thrown one upon the other by their captors.

Tex saw a scuffle still going on, then saw the gold-threaded *agal* of Sheik 'brahim. He was raging at the indignity of being physically handled; he, a sheik by his own right and the son of a sheik. He was fighting furiously, recklessly — bravely.

But in time he was thrown back with the panting legionnaires, with Mahfra, clinging to the American girl, and ex-Nazi Sturmer. Tex caught him as he crashed back among them. He called: 'Take it easy, brother. They've slipped one over us.'

'brahim shouted fiercely: 'That dog of a cur from the bazaars did it! Is it not as I said? Did he not plan treachery?'

Tex stood up, holding back the irate patrician Arab. It seemed to be as 'brahim said.

Suleiman was standing back from

them, big and ugly in his scarecrow clothes. He was holding his hands to his eyes, as if they were in pain, and men were standing about him, holding wet cloths for his face and earthenware bowls of water for drinking. Plainly Suleiman was among friends, and they were concerned for his plight and were trying to ease his discomfort.

Tex thought: 'It must have been hell for him, having to find the way for our party up that defile, in all that glare.' But his thoughts weren't charitable towards the man any longer.

They had saved Suleiman's life, and it seemed he had betrayed them. In that instant, looking at those fierce men around him, Tex felt the extent of that betrayal.

It would involve his death, and the death of all his companions.

Tex let his eyes wander over the men who filled the cavern now. There must have been thirty or forty of them. They were all dressed much as Suleiman was dressed, in ragged *galabier* and wearing the knitted skullcaps or turbans rather than the *kafir* that was traditional to the

Bedouin of those parts.

It made him think: 'They're out of their place here. These are no nomads. These are town beggars.' And he wondered what they were doing here, four hundred miles from the nearest Arab town of size.

They were an assorted lot, some tall, some short, a few of them plump and even fat, but mostly lean men. It was only when he came to look at their faces that he found the common thread that bound them together.

And that was the look of torment in their eyes.

He saw some who were physically affected, like Suleiman the Hideous, whose face had been so brutally changed. But many, when he looked, seemed normal men in appearance, some of the younger ones appearing to be strong, intelligent and good-looking, and without marks of torture. But when he caught their gaze he knew that they too had suffered, though they had no wounds to show for it. Perhaps their suffering had been on a mental, rather than a physical, plane.

His tongue clacked dryly in his head. In

his desire for water he could even forget the danger that hemmed them in. He started to push his way forward, through the ranks of those silent Arabs, heading for the water that the horses were enjoying.

He shouted to his companions: 'There's water here. Come on; let's get it!'

His action had a curious effect upon the Arabs. They yielded to his pushing, letting him go on towards the water; for it is instinctive with an Arab to permit even a deadly enemy an opportunity to allay a thirst.

But they jostled along with the ex-legionnaires and their Arab companions, forming a circle that ringed them round even when they went plunging into the water, so that there was no possibility of escape.

Nicky was clinging to his hand, so that Tex and the girl ran into the cool, sparkling water together. The relief was instantaneous; the swift-running water seemed to drain away the fire that consumed their bodies even before they began to drink.

They stooped, reckless of water wetting

their clothes, burying their heads in the cool, glassy-surfaced liquid and drinking in great greedy choking gulps. It was salty, but quite drinkable.

In time they were satisfied. Then the life seemed to go out of their limbs and they wanted only to rest. They dragged themselves back to the rocky bank and sank at the feet of their captors.

For a time they were content to rest there, and the silent Arabs ringing them made no move to disturb them. Tex used his eyes. He saw how the water came coursing down a smooth-worn channel in the rock, emptying from a hole that was a big, black eye let into the rock face of the mountain. The smooth-running stream rippled round a bend and disappeared from sight, apparently tunnelling through the great white wall of salt that rimmed the cavern.

His head turned and his weary eyes looked towards the entrance to this mighty cave, carved through aeons of time from out the mountain of salt. It was a large opening, through which the bright sunlight came reflecting from that valley of clean white salt outside.

Tex thought: 'This is a wonderful hiding place.' And then he wondered why the Brotherhood of Tormented Men had come to it, why they needed a hiding place.

He saw Sturmer moving away from the party, doing it covertly, his eyes on Tex. When the ex-Nazi found that Tex was looking at him, he paused for a moment, but then, as if in defiance, began to resume his way almost immediately.

Tex rapped: 'Where d'you think you're going?' — coming to his feet immediately. Sturmer didn't answer him. Instead he came erect and walked through the circle of Arabs towards where Suleiman squatted on the ground, his head resting on his folded arms. Evidently Suleiman was suffering from that exposure up the Valley-where-men-go-blind.

Sturmer, his cissy, rimless eyeglasses flashing light as his small, sallow face jerked round to look at Tex, towering above the Arabs, knelt by the side of their former guide and began to talk to him in Arabic. Tex shoved his way across. He wanted to know what this devil was

90

proposing to Suleiman.

He saw Sully's head lift a little, and move as if answering the Legion captain, though his face didn't rise above the tattered sleeves of his *galabier*. Sturmer came closer, talking urgently.

Tex found a great, rising rage within him. Rage against this man whose life they had saved at peril to their own . . . rage against Sturmer who might use his tongue to save his own worthless life while they lost theirs. His temper snapped and he went jumping forward, hands clawing. Nicky screamed, afraid that he would bring quick disaster upon himself, but he ignored the cry.

Sturmer came leaping to his feet, his face bitter with hate Then Tex saw something flash in his hand, and realised that Sturmer had all the time been in possession of some weapon unknown to the legionnaires.

It was a knife.

Tex heard a gabble of excited cries from the Arabs. There was a savage, rising exultation to it, as if they thrilled to the thought that two of their hated European oppressors would provide a gory spectacle for them.

Suleiman's head jerked up at the cry. Tex had a vision of that hideous, yet intelligent face; he saw the eyes screwed up in pain, and in that moment he thought, almost with shock: 'Sully suffered a lot to bring us through to water.'

Then Sturmer was plunging in towards him, cork-screwing through the air, his hand going back and then stabbing forward with incredible rapidity. Tex saw the gleaming blade ripping towards his chest, and again heard that terrified scream from Nicky.

He let himself go — let his legs buckle so that his body fell sideways and yet fell forward. The blade stabbed air, just behind his back. Next moment Sturmer's vicious satisfaction changed to alarm . . . and pain.

That big, steel-hard body of the Texan crashed into Sturmer's legs, and Sturmer went face down on to the rock too suddenly for him to break his fall.

Tex rolled clear. The Arabs were crowding round, their eyes big and excited, their mouths open in savage encouragement. These men who had suffered so much now wanted to see other suffer, and it was all the better because the contestants wore the hated blue uniform of the French Foreign Legion.

Nicky and the others were fighting their way through, and Tex caught a momentary glimpse of the American girl's horrified face — then saw the quick change to relief when she realised that Tex was not hurt.

He came to his feet, crouching, his hand going instinctively to his belt for his revolver, but that had been snatched from him when they had dragged him from his horse. He faced Sturmer, who was staggering to his feet, still clutching that small but deadly knife.

Sturmer's glasses had somehow, miraculously, stayed on his nose. It made him look ridiculous, a prissily be-glassed man holding a stabbing knife in his hand, and yet somehow it also made him look the more deadly, the more venomous. Tex didn't allow himself to be deceived by those glasses, anyway.

As Sturmer came leaping back, his Arab head-dress floating behind him at the sudden movement, Tex went rocking forward, his body swaying to deceive his opponent. Sturmer started to lunge again, and found his opponent was going the other way. His thin lips opened in a snarl of rage, and with incredible swiftness he came teetering round to strike again at the big Texan.

And Tex crashed helplessly at the ex-Nazi's feet, his legs entangling with the ragged gown of Suleiman, unable to get out of the way of the contestants.

Tex rolled over frantically, fighting to get his boots out of the clinging, holding folds. He saw Suleiman's face near to his own, jerking round to look at something, saw his eyes open wide though he seemed to do it with an effort, as if forcing them open against pain.

The shouting from the Arabs was deafening suddenly, reverberating in the close confines of that high-roofed cavern. Tex rolled again, and his feet came free. Sturmer was crashing straight down towards his unprotected body, triumph blazing on that small, sallow face, that gleaming blade already beginning to descend towards him.

Then the bare foot of Suleiman, like an enormous horny plate, came stabbing up into Sturmer's stomach. Sturmer fell on to that stiffly-outstretched leg; his weight carried him forward, so that he went flying over their heads and landed on the rocky floor a second time.

Tex began to scramble to his feet — then his movements slowed. Sturmer had knocked himself out with that fall.

The ex-cattle rancher from Texas stood erect, wiping his perspiring forehead with the back of his tunic sleeve. He looked at Suleiman. Sully had rolled sideways and was again covering his eyes against the light. The way he lay, curled stiffly under his rags, told of the pain he was suffering. Tex wondered if the man was going blind from his ordeal of traversing that valley in the full light of the Sahara sun.

As he stood, trying to get his breath, he saw that the crowd was beginning to break up, talking excitedly and laughing a lot, no doubt going over the details of that brief brawl. And many looked angry and disappointed, their eyes telling of the desire in them to see even greater violence.

It was strange, but his companions didn't come near him. Nicky was crying, probably from relief at seeing him safe for the moment, and this time it was the Arab girl, Mahfra, who came and put her arm round her to comfort her.

He thought: 'Nicky can't stand much more of this sort of thing.' She was tough, as all newspaperwomen must be tough, but her brand of toughness after all didn't usually lead to participation in savage fighting, or the risking of her life as she had been doing lately. She was breaking under the strain, mental and physical.

He shrugged, yet he wasn't indifferent. There was just nothing he could do about it.

His eyes turned towards Sturmer. There was one among those Tormented Men who could still find compassion in his heart. Now he came forward with a crudely-baked earthenware bowl containing water and began to bathe the bruised forehead of the unconscious Sturmer. He was a little old man, devoid of any pretensions to looks.

Some of the Arabs grew angry and called querulously for him to leave the accursed infidel to himself, but the old man just went on bathing that small, white face of the man who had never shown mercy in his life.

A tall, young-looking Arab had detached himself from the crowd and was standing close by the recumbent Suleiman now. He was a handsome man, more like a Greek in his face than an Arab, and telling of the mixed blood that is the heritage of Moslem Africa.

Tex didn't have to be told that here was the leader of this Brotherhood, united by the pain that had once been common to them all.

They looked at each other, tall Arab and tall Texan. Two fine, strong, leaders of men. The Arab saw a lean, hard-looking face with eyes that yet spoke of softer emotions . . . the face of an intelligent man.

Tex saw a finely-shaped head, with crisp black curly hair; a face that a sculptor or artist would have delighted in, so perfectly proportioned was it. He met those cool, thoughtful eyes and decided: 'This fellar's got a brain.'

He was leader of that Brotherhood, yet it seemed to Tex that he was the youngest man there. He marvelled at it, but he puzzled also over one curious fact.

This man had never known torment. No man with such calm eyes could have been brutally treated and remained like this. Yet he was the leader of the Brotherhood of Tormented Men.

The Greek-like Arab was speaking softly down at Suleiman, for all he looked at Tex. Tex didn't get the question, but he caught fragments of Suleiman's reply.

' . . . didn't trust me. Afraid to travel after dark . . . Had to bring them . . . dangerous . . . mustn't let them escape.'

Tex sighed and strolled forward, his feet echoing with a curious hollow sound on that rocky flooring. He lowered himself by the side of Suleiman. The leader of the Brotherhood just stood where he was, watching down upon the pair.

Tex said, gently: 'What's in your mind,

Sully? I mean, what're you. plannin' for us?'

Suleiman never moved, never said anything. Just lay crouching there in pain. The Arab leader never spoke, either.

So Tex said: 'You don't need to tell me. You aim to wipe us out, don't you? You had to bring us with you, because you couldn't get away from us, not after that first time when I caught you tryin' to mount a hoss.'

He'd never told his companions about that attempt, he remembered.

'You're scared of us, because we know your hide-out. You figger we might betray you.' To whom? He didn't know.

At that Suleiman stirred. His head came peering up from the folds of his *galabier*. His face looked more revolting than ever, because his eyes were red-rimmed from suffering.

Suleiman said, tiredly: 'No, Tex. The crime you have committed against the Brotherhood is that you know it exists. You spoke about it to me, you and your companions. No man must know — not yet awhile — that there is a Brotherhood;

and we can trust no one.'

He shrugged.

'Besides, I do not know how much my blabbing tongue told you in the night. Perhaps you know more than you spoke of to me.'

Tex was looking across at his companions. They, too, had settled on to the stone floor. They were grouped together, looking his way, as if, he thought, they were depending on him to get them out of this mess.

Sturmer was sitting up now, though he was too dazed to realise what had happened to him. He had lost his glasses in that last fall, and was peering around him like an owl in daylight. That compassionate Arab seemed to understand his loss and hunted around until he found the precious glasses. Sturmer was in luck; they hadn't been broken.

Other Arabs were making a fire out of dried dung down nearer to the entrance of the cave.

Tex said: 'It's a fine thing, to reward us this way. You'd be dead now, Sully, but for us.' Yet he didn't feel anger any more against Suleiman the Hideous. He had a feeling that the actions of this curious man were neither narrow nor selfish, however ruthless they seemed.

Suleiman answered simply: 'It is not a thing I wish to do, but our lives are little compared with the misery and distress of a continent of afflicted people. The Brotherhood is preparing to help these people, to take away the whips and chains and branding irons of their oppressors — aye, to remove the oppressors themselves. You, unfortunately, might betray us — perhaps inadvertently, perhaps unwillingly — but the betrayal would be the same and the consequences no less unfortunate for the people we plan to help.'

His head went back into the folds of his gown. At that the tall young Arab who looked so like a Greek god, knelt, his hand lightly patting the shoulder of his comrade. He spoke, in the Arabic of the Nile, and his voice was deep and rich and like music, for all the guttural dialect he used.

'Suleiman the Good,' he almost intoned, and there was affection in his voice. 'He has the headache,' he said, looking at Tex with a smile on his handsome face. 'But it will soon go.'

Tex listened again to those city accents, and then he asked: 'Why are you here, you and your Brotherhood? You're not of the desert; you're townspeople, city dwellers.'

'Most of us,' agreed the young Arab leader. 'And we come from Baghdad and Basra, from Tehran, Beirut and Damascus. You'll find a man among us from Amman, in Transjordan, from Yemen down the Gulf, where men still lose their hands if they are driven by hunger to steal. We come from every part of the Arab-speaking world, united by the suffering that is common to us all, and thirsting only for the day when we can strike back at our oppressors.'

'You,' said Tex levelly, 'have never known suffering.'

The Arab inclined his head in assent. 'That is true. But I have seen it, have watched my fellows suffer all the days of my life. I have imagination and can feel the horrors without the need for actual experience.'

Tex shook his head, looking into that fine, patrician face. His own voice sounded harsh as he sought for Arabic to express his views. 'Imagination is a poor substitute for experience. Unless you've suffered, brother, you'll never be as they are — never, in the end, so determined, never so . . . reliable.'

Suleiman's ugly face was coming out from the folds of his gown, his peering eyes looking towards his leader, as if looking for something he had never suspected before. The young Arab patted his shoulder, as if to reassure his follower, a smile on his face.

'Perhaps you are right, O Americano. But perhaps I am the exception; I can see suffering and can feel it.' His hand suddenly went to his heart, yet he remained unemotional in spite of the gesture. His fine eyes were as calm as ever; here was no man to indulge in histrionics even to establish a point.

He said, gently: 'Do you know what I have seen? I have seen men and women and children die of diseases — in an agony as great or greater than any that could be inflicted on a battlefield. Yet almost all of those deadly sicknesses are preventable; there is the knowledge, and the money to buy that knowledge, but our rulers seek fit to dissipate it . . . and so always poor people die.

'I have seen men — aye, and women, too — taken from their homes and incarcerated in terrifying prisons and there brutally treated because they had questioned the need for this way of life, so unfair to the majority, to the people least able to look after themselves.'

His hand gestured, indicating his companions. Tex saw that it was a good hand, slim and smooth and unmarked by toil.

'Every year men who have the courage to raise their voices against a barbarous system ebb out their lives in a bath of pain somewhere where no man can help them — somewhere inhabited only by fellow-unfortunates and the brutes who inflict tortures upon them. Sometimes it seems even these fiends weary of tormenting men, and then a few are allowed to crawl away from the torture chambers. Then, if their spirits are still resolute, they join us in this work which is to rid the world of sadists and self-seekers.'

Tex rose. Almost he could be humorous at that moment. He said: 'Much more of that, friend, and I'll be going gladly towards whatever fate is in store for me.'

Then he asked again: 'But why come here? Why have you come from all parts of the Arab-speaking world? What is the mission of the Brotherhood in North Africa?'

Suleiman the Hideous spoke, the cloth of his *galabier* to his eyes. 'Because though all men suffer, yet there is ignorance of the cause of this suffering. It is only necessary for our oppressors to say: 'Follow me', and they go blindly after them, into any madness.'

Tex looked down, those words suddenly becoming significant. His memory flitted over the events of the past few days.

'War,' he said softly. 'That's what's brought you here, isn't it?'

They didn't answer, but he knew he

was right. Once again the Arabs had risen against the French in North Africa. They had captured and sacked — by treachery on the part of some of the garrison, admittedly — the French outpost in the desert at El Kwatra. Tex and his companions had escaped from the post only just in time.

Later, in their attempt to escape across the desert, they had witnessed a battle between Arab Nationalists and a strong force of Legion and Colonial troops. They didn't know the result, but it had been a bloody battle at an oasis whose name they did not even know.

The uprising had been instigated by Sheik Mahmoud ibn Hussein el Dusa, though he was a man with many other names. A thin man, ever-humourless, suspicious and belligerent and always seeking power. Tex had disliked the man at sight — and had liked him no better when the sheik sent men to get his, Tex's, head.

With the start of the uprising, Nuhas Pasha had come to take charge of the Arab army. Abdul el Nuhas was a legendary name in North Africa, for had he not been the fiercest fighter against the corrupt and mismanaging French until his final defeat and exile in Egypt? With his coming the revolt had been changed from another desert uprising to that of a war.

Men had come flocking to his standard from all parts of North Africa, even from Libya and Egypt itself, such was the magnetism of the war-leader's name.

Tex had met Nuhas Pasha, a bold, handsome, middle-aged Arab sheik, of considerable culture and charm. A man very different from the bitter, malevolent Sheik Mahmoud el Dusa, who had with reluctance handed over command of the army on Nuhas Pasha's arrival.

So now the American rubbed a button absentmindedly between his lean brown fingers and said: 'Nuhas Pasha . . . he came over the Border from Egypt only a few days ago. I reckon you fellars came here after him.'

Suleiman said nothing, but kept his head down on his knees. The Arab leader didn't speak, either; instead a tiny smile came to his face, as if he were saying to himself: 'You don't get me to answer questions. Not when I've decided I've said enough.' And it seemed he had decided he had said enough.

Tex nodded. He felt sure of the connection himself. He looked down at Suleiman. He wanted to know what their plans were, how a desert war affected the Brotherhood. The Greek-like Arab seemed able to read his thoughts. Tex saw another good-humoured smile come to that face, and then heard him say: 'My friend, you have asked enough questions about us. Already you know too much. It is unfortunate . . . ' He shrugged.

Tex looked across at his friends. These were remarkable men. Their liking for him seemed sincere, yet it made no difference to them. He and his friends knew enough, seemingly, to perhaps throw all the plans of the Brotherhood into discord — they could upset this grandiose scheme to bring relief to suffering Arab millions. For that they must be silenced.

He said, dryly: 'Gee, brother, I'm sorry we're goin' to upset you.' Abruptly he asked: 'When's it goin' to happen?'

Suleiman lifted his head at that, peering into the face of his leader. His manner seemed to repeat the question.

The young Arab shrugged. Tex heard him murmur: 'Not here . . . outside.'

'We'd spoil the look of the place.' Tex spoke cynically. Sure, they couldn't have corpses lying around. Easier to ride them out into the desert and then —

Suleiman spoke broodingly. He seemed less troubled by his eyes now, as if they were recovering. 'That means after sundown.'

Tex's eyes looked at the sunlight beyond the cave entrance. It was still very bright, too bright even for an execution party to face. He thought: 'While there's sunshine we live.' And it was ironical; for only a short while ago the sunshine had been killing them, this sunshine that gave them respite now.

The Arab leader looked at the girls with the ex-legionnaires and the sullen young sheik. He said, softly: 'I regret the unpleasantness. Regret it especially because you seem a worthy man, one who could be of the Tormented Men. But — ' Again that expressive shrug of those square-set shoulders under the nightgown-like garment that didn't look ridiculous on the young Arab.

His glance came back to Tex. 'They do not need to know,' he said significantly.

Both began to walk across to where Tex's friends awaited him.

'Meanin'?' Tex didn't catch on.

'You are a man of generous heart. There is no need for their last hours to be troubled.' Their eyes met. 'If you wished to spare them agony, you could tell them you were to be led back to the desert, with full waterskins, after dark. They would never know . . . '

It was a strange proposition from the young fanatic, but suddenly Tex nodded. He thought: 'Why not? Why make 'em worry?' And he also thought, determinedly: 'Maybe I'll get a chance to make a break for it . . . we might somehow turn the tables on 'em.'

While there was life there was hope. Only now, he remembered, looking at that bright patch of sunlight, it was a case of. 'While there's light there's hope.'

He made up his mind and walked across to his friends. That curious old man who had shown compassion towards the fallen Sturmer was with his party, holding a shallow wooden bowl in which was a little chopped meat stewed up with vegetables. There wasn't much for such a number, but then that old, old man went back and got them some new-baked *koubes*, that brown, unleavened bread of the Arab.

As Tex strode across, they all looked up at him, their eyes holding him — holding him in a way he didn't like. He had to turn his head as if interested in the tattered throng who squatted nearer to the cave entrance, where the cooking fire smouldered and filled the air with a curious, acrid, almost incense-like odour.

For now he was having to lie to them, and he didn't like having to do that.

He lowered himself on to the cool rock, sitting close against Nicky. He felt her hands clasp around his arm, and it was flattering, for he felt the relief that came to her because she could feel his strength through that coarse blue material.

He said: 'Looks like we might get away with things, after all.'

They all looked at him, with pathetic eagerness. Joe Ellighan with his flat, battered pan; Rube the Pole who had become American, his face bright and apple red as it always was — 'brahim, suspicion even now clouding his relief, and Mahfra of the dark loveliness. Sturmer was sitting against the salt wall, his eyes not looking at anything.

Nicky almost whispered: 'Oh, Tex, what do you mean?'

'Just that.' He gave a grin, and hoped it looked more natural than it felt on him. 'When the sunshine goes off the salt slopes outside an' it's safe enough to walk with our eyes open, we're gonna be led out with full waterskins.'

'Oh, thank goodness!' Nicky almost wept. 'I thought — '

'Sure, we all thought they hadn't good intentions towards us. But — wal, I reckon they don't like strangers.'

Nicky said: 'I misjudged Suleiman. This will be a lesson to me. Never again will I judge a man by his face.'

'Sure, honey, I reckon Suleiman was misjudged by someone.' Tex's voice sounded tired. He was thinking: 'Yeah, I was that someone. All the others had him taped, but me, Big-head, I had to know better.'

He looked at Suleiman, standing now and talking to his chief, and he wished that he had left him to die in the desert. Or shot him out of hand, that time he'd caught him trying to repay generosity by running off with a horse.

But now it was too late. He lay back, pillowing his head on Nicky's soft lap. She held him as if she loved to hold him so close to her.

His friends stretched themselves, to sleep after the trying day, suddenly reassured by what Tex had told them. Before, sleep had been impossible because of the worry of their situation, but now they found they couldn't keep their eyes open. After a few minutes Tex found the girl drooping over him, falling asleep where she sat. He rolled away and caught her as she fell. She didn't waken, and went on sleeping when he cradled her in his arms.

Only Tex didn't immediately sleep. His eyes couldn't leave that bright patch of sunshine that told him how long he had to live. To his weary eyes it seemed that he could see a perceptible diminishment in the brightness of the sun's rays. And there was a shadow that began to grow at astonishing speed from a hidden salt peak towards the right of the cave entrance.

Once again he looked towards Suleiman and the Arab leader. They were sitting together, conversing softly. The young Arab caught his eye. At once he stopped speaking, smiled and nodded. It was incongruous, that friendliness when their lives were running out, and by order of that very young man.

6

Back to the Legion

Next thing Tex knew, he was being wakened from sleep. It seemed fantastic, impossible, that sleep could have come to him, with that threat of death marching steadily towards them, and yet he must have dozed off.

He sat up. There was a stir and bustle about the cavern now, as if in preparation for some unusual event. He saw tattered *galabiers* flying, bony ankles skipping around, as the Brotherhood went rounding up the horses and filling goatskins from the smooth-running stream.

There was a lot of talk from the men, and it was pitched in a rather high key, so that for the moment there was the illusion of pleasant excitement, and it was this chatter that had wakened him.

He saw Suleiman, no longer holding his eyes, standing back a dozen yards and watching them where they slept. He remembered, and his eyes shot round towards that cavern entrance . . .

The light was still there, but no longer was it glowing with direct reflection from the sun. He thought, panic welling: 'The sun's already down. Darkness will be here soon. Right now we can leave, can be led out to our deaths.'

Even now preparations were afoot for the final journey into the desert. That excitement was the essential accompaniment to a preparation for murder, he realised.

Nicky was stirring. She woke, caught his eye and smiled. It had refreshed her, this long sleep in the cool cavern, and she looked better than she had been for some time. She was happy, too, feeling safe, and her smile was almost joyous as she awoke and met his gaze.

'Hello, Tex,' he heard her whisper. 'I think I was dreaming about you.' Those blue eyes laughed at him. He felt it had been a pleasant dream.

Then Rube came awake, looking fresh and alert immediately. Tex wondered how he could do it, but Rube the Schemer was always like that.

He awoke with some scheme turning nimbly in his brain, as if he had been working things out in his sleep.

'You know what?' he asked, the minute he realised that Tex was sitting there and in a position to listen to him. 'You know, I reckon we ought to have kept goin' south towards Lake Chad.'

Tex almost groaned. It had been Rube's idea to desert and head south through the African continent towards Lake Chad, and territory administered by the British. His argument had been that that was the last place anyone would expect deserters to go, and so they would be safe from pursuit.

'brahim had changed their plans for them, however, by offering to lead them to a Libyan port. It was nearer, much nearer, and he'd guaranteed them safe escort through Arab country. Now, Tex realised, Rube was still hankering after the more grandiose scheme, of taking the long trail into Central Africa.

'You like to do things the hard way,' he

growled. He didn't feel like arguing. The way things were, there was neither Lake Chad nor a Libyan port ahead for them. Just a short ride into the desert, where their rotting carcases wouldn't foul the Brotherhood's living quarters. And then? He shrugged. The Arabs hadn't returned them their Lebels. No doubt they were to die by rifle fire — from their own rifles.

Ex-legionnaire Joe Ellighan came out of his sleep just then. His good-humoured, battered face split into a smile. 'Guess we got the woist over,' he yapped. 'Reckon now there ain't nuttin' to stop us between here and de coast.'

Rube said: 'A mere four hundred miles of desert,' but the way he said it, Tex knew he was wishing the distance was over a thousand miles — to his beloved Lake Chad.

'brahim walked across to the stream in stately manner; his burnouse closely held about him, and knelt and drank. When he had finished he stayed where he was, watching the preparations for the ride out. Tex tried to see his face, but the folds of his hooded cloak hid it for the moment. He was never sure about 'brahim; 'brahim seemed to see things and to understand situations before most men.

Abruptly Tex looked at Mahfra. The Arab girl was still lying on her side, but she was awake and looking past the Texan. He saw that expression of wide-eyed horror on her lovely young face, and knew what it signified.

When he looked quickly over his shoulder, he saw that Suleiman was looking at the girl. Suleiman wanted her; that was why he couldn't keep his eyes off her. And the girl had known it from the first, and was appalled that she should have attracted the interest of Suleiman the Hideous.

Tex rose, wanting to break the spell cast by Suleiman's fascinated gaze. He began to walk across the rocky cavern floor towards the Arab who had led them to their death — or that was how it seemed. Nicky came after him, and he wasn't sure he wanted her to be with him in this conversation with Suleiman. But he could only smile when she slipped her arm through his, and held it tightly, almost exultantly. They hadn't spoken of love, except obliquely jocularly, but each knew of the feelings of the other.

Nicky was happy. Tex sighed and changed the words of condemnation that had been on his lips. Instead he gave the customary Arab greeting: 'God is great.'

Suleiman's brown eyes regarded him thoughtfully. Then, speaking in the English that was so tinged with a Scottish accent, he said, courteously: 'It is time for you to leave us. May god go with you.'

Tex nodded. 'Yeah, I reckon it's time,' he agreed. The light was fading, where the white salt valley showed through the entrance of the cave.

'Your waterskins are filled ready for the journey. Food is in your saddlebags. You will mount and ride out within a few minutes, while there is yet light enough to see along that Valley-where-men-go-blind.'

The horses were being led towards his friends, he saw. He just nodded and turned to go. He felt sick. It was hard to pretend to be composed with a man who was planning their murder. He would have liked to have thrown himself on the fellow, and at least hurt him before he went out. It wouldn't do any good, he knew, but it was a natural reaction to treachery . . .

But Nicky was there, and Nicky was happy. There was no need to spoil her last moments on earth, so he kept quiet. He looked towards the blue uniforms of Rube and Joe Ellighan. When he could, he intended to speak to them, to warn them, and get them to follow him if he tried to make a break for freedom.

Astonished, suddenly he heard Nicky speaking, her voice so clear in that empty hollowness of this cave of salt . . . astonished because of the words she was speaking, and because they were addressed to the man she had instinctively decided was their enemy.

'Sully, I want to apologise to you.' Resolutely she was facing up to the man who so merited the title of Hideous. 'I — I misjudged you and I want to say I'm sorry. I thought all along you weren't to be trusted, but it seems you are — that you're helping us. So . . . sorry I thought bad things against you, Sully.'

There was the most friendly, comradely smile on her face. Tex wanted to pull her away, to shout: 'He isn't worth it. He isn't planning to help us. Don't harbour nice thoughts about this — this rattlesnake!'

But all he could do was take her arm now and try to pull her away. She resisted, and he had to stand by her side. Suleiman was watching her fair face, that looked so much the fairer because of the dark skins around her. Tex couldn't read the man's thoughts, but he felt that Suleiman was not at ease, receiving those impetuous thanks.

Nicky was speaking again, words tumbling from her lips in her gratefulness, and in repentance for having entertained unworthy thoughts about this dignified beggar-like creature.

'I'd like to help you, Sully.' Her blue eyes were searching that scarred and ugly face. She was a wise girl, this newspaperwoman, and often saw what others failed to observe. And she hadn't missed Suleiman's interest in Mahfra.

'I know what you want, Sully — more

than anything in the world. And I know what's between you and your desire.'

Suleiman's eyes were blank, but they didn't move from the American girl's face.

'You — you want to be like other men, don't you?' Nicky's voice was softer, understanding, sympathetic. 'You . . . want a wife of your own.'

Suleiman answered honestly, his voice suddenly breaking in on her speech. 'I want a woman. Why shouldn't I? I'm no different from other men.'

'But there is a barrier — '

'What woman will come to the arms of a man with a face like mine?' demanded Suleiman savagely, and it was the first time that Tex had heard his voice in anything but equable mood. The Arab half-turned, as if the rising frustration in him demanded movement, however small it was.

Nicky said: 'Men made your face like that, Sully, and men can remake it.' She was talking about plastic surgery, Tex knew. 'Sully, just now I feel so grateful to you, after my suspicions, that I will commit myself with a promise. Come with us and I will write about you in my paper, and generous people will help you to have the treatment that will make you look a normal man again.'

Tex pulled her away at that, leaving Suleiman standing, his face averted — but thinking.

He demanded, savagely: 'Why did you have to say all that?'

Nicky was indignant. 'You don't seem grateful — '

'Why should I be? We got into this jam through pouring our precious water into his ugly pan.'

'You shouldn't talk like that about him.' Nicky halted, astonished at his unfriend-liness. 'I don't understand you. Why, Tex, all along you're the one who's been friendliest towards Sully. You seem to have changed . . . '

Tex walked away quickly. He didn't want to talk with her, because he felt that he wouldn't be able to keep up this awful pretence much longer. He wanted to speak with Joe and Rube, anyway.

He looked round for Sturmer. He

couldn't see him. But with all that bustle of Arabs around the horses, no doubt the Nazi was hidden from sight.

Joe and Rube were attending to the girths of their mounts. 'brahim was already in the saddle, impatient to ride out, his aristocratic features showing the haughty contempt he felt for this ragged mob about him. He was no diplomat with his features, Tex thought, and wished that he, Tex, could show his own boiling viciousness. But he couldn't.

The light was fading inside the cave. He jerked his head, to get his comrades away from the listening ears of the crowding Arabs. They came out, Joe perspiring from his exertions.

But when the three former legionnaires grouped together suddenly the Greek god-like Arab leader was standing with them. He was smiling as he met Tex's eyes. Tex thought: 'He doesn't intend me to warn the boys.'

For a moment he deliberated, then decided to postpone the attempt. Maybe in a moment or two he'd have chance to tell their of the fate intended when they rode through that white valley on to the desert outside.

Instead he asked: 'Where's Sturmer? I don't see him.'

The Arab said: 'The officer? He stays here.'

Tex grabbed him, his manner fierce. 'He's my prisoner,' he rapped. Instantly Arabs were crowding round to support their leader; all in one second the legionnaires found themselves the centre of an angry-eyed mob.

The Arab leader merely continued his smile and pushed Tex away from him. 'You're forgetting,' was all he said. 'You won't need Sturmer now . . . '

Tex had forgotten.

The Arab shrugged expressively. 'He is an officer in the service of France. There is much that he can tell us — more than unwilling legionnaires, for instance.' His voice became soft. 'When you are gone, we intend to make him talk.' His hand jerked towards the horses, his tone suddenly authoritative. 'Mount — and ride. It is easier to negotiate that valley while there is still some light.'

Tex's eyes reluctantly left that handsome face and went instead to the Arabs who surrounded them. The legionnaires' own Lebel rifles were in those brown, clutching hands, and the barrels were pointing towards them.

He shrugged and began to push his way towards the horses, Nicky and the others at his heels. He felt the bewilderment of his companions, especially of Nicky. By now they must have sensed there was something unusual in the atmosphere.

When they were seated on their horses, Rube spoke, and Tex knew he was testing the honesty of these Arabs. 'Okay, brothers, now we're ready to ride. You've got my rifle, Abdul — '

The smiling Arab leader said swiftly, smoothly: 'Your rifles will be handed to you when you are through the valley. But not here.'

He didn't say why. Rube looked suddenly into Tex's grim, grey eyes. He was tumbling to things, thought Tex. Rube was a smart boy. He felt glad that Rube's suspicions were being alerted;

they might have need of his quick wits very soon now He saw Rube pull his horse up against Joe Ellighan's. He must have said something in an undertone, without opening his mouth, for Joe's big head jerked up in astonishment, and his battered face came round to look at Suleiman.

The horses began to string out, Tex's leading the way, led by one of the Arabs. The other Arabs fell in on either side of the mounts. They were carrying more arms now than he'd noticed before, though apart from their Lebel rifles, they hadn't much in the way of guns.

He heard Nicky, speaking from the horse behind him. He thought: 'She's trying to dissipate this ugly little atmosphere that's developed.' She was still wanting to atone for her previous suspicions of Suleiman — the man who now appeared about to lead them on their way again.

'Are you coming with us, Sully?' Her tone was significant. She was hinting at the promise she had previously made.

Suleiman's voice, calm and steady:

'Only as far as the desert.'

'You're not going to take advantage of my . . . offer?'

'No.' Almost he could imagine that ugly, cropped head shaking with the negative. 'I am grateful to you for your generosity. I would like to take advantage of it. But there is work for me among the Brotherhood, and I must not think of myself, but only of the people who need me.'

Tex's head came round at that. He looked at Suleiman and saw the honesty on the man's face. This man had a mission in life, and he was not to be swerved from it by anything.

He was a fanatic, of course, yet Tex was beginning to realise that the man's mission was humanitarian, even noble, for all that he could send them, apparently unmoved, to their death.

'Some day, perhaps, I will seek out these doctors who can make a new man of me.' There was a curious, twisted smile on Suleiman's features. 'Just now I will adopt other measures to satisfy my desires.'

He said it so easily, so casually, that it passed without impinging on their consciousness. It was only later — a few moments later — that they remembered those words, and remembered them with horror and loathing.

They were right up to the entrance of the cavern now. Tex saw that night was not far away, and the whiteness of the salt mountains was softened and long shadows stretched in deep, dark pools to break the surface.

He was riding out into a night air that was hot because it came eddying over a desert that was saturated with a day's intense heat, when suddenly there was a shout from behind. He wheeled instantly, his hands seeking instinctively for a gun — and finding nothing.

'brahim was raging, far behind them. Some of the Brotherhood were holding his horse, and he was striking at them and kicking out with his sandalled feet. Tex shouted above the hubbub: 'What's the matter, 'brahim?'

Rube got the message and relayed it. It brought them all wheeling swiftly back on their horses to where the Arab sheik was held, though the men on the reins tried to hold them back.

'Mahfra is not to come with us!'

There was a mighty confusion then, with everyone shouting at the top of their voices, and the huge cavern echoing back their words, magnifying and distorting them. Tex saw Suleiman and the leader of the Brotherhood, standing back from the crowd.

He shouted: 'Where's Mahfra? We don't go without her!'

A roar went up from his companions. 'Just gimme a rifle,' he could hear Elly yapping. Horses were rearing and kicking in fright, while bearded, tattered-gowned Arabs clung tenaciously on to their heads. Everywhere men were shouting and scattering in alarm, only to form into a big circle when safely out of range of those flying hooves.

Suleiman and his leader kept going backwards before Tex's prancing horse.

'Mahfra!' 'brahim was shouting, but there was no answer from anywhere along that big cavern.

Suleiman lifted his hands. It took a full half minute, though, before there was silence enough to hear what the man had to say.

Then Suleiman replied: 'O Teksuss, it is in my heart to keep the Arab girl, for she is not of your kind — ' and then he looked at 'brahim, contemptuously — 'nor of your kind, either. She is of the *fellahin*, a peasant girl, and she pleases me and I want her.'

'But she doesn't want you!' 'brahim, furious.

'Perhaps some day she will be glad she had me and not a sheik brought up to believe in many women,' Suleiman replied significantly.

Tex raged and shouted: 'We want that gal, Suleiman. Fetch her at once, or — '

'Or what?' demanded that Arab leader, stepping between Suleiman and the enraged American. He was smiling pleasantly.

Tex looked down the muzzles of rifles, a few of them their own Lebels. He remembered their helplessness, and swallowed.

Then Suleiman's voice came softly to his ears, and he was sure that none of the others heard it. 'This way O Tek-suss, her life will be saved . . . '

Those words turned off his anger like the twisting of a tap. His eyes looked into Suleiman's, and it seemed there was pleading in them, pleading for understanding.

Ex-Legionnaire Texas understood.

He wheeled his horse. 'Okay,' he said to his companions. 'Let's go.'

'And leave Mahfra?' Nicky was quivering with horror and indignation.

'D'you know any argument agen them guns?' Tex put all the cynicism he could into his question. Yet in the end the logic of what he said was unanswerable. In the end they had to move before the threat of those blued barrels.

Dispirited and crestfallen, stunned and bewildered by events that seemed without logical explanation, the tiny cavalcade went out into the gathering darkness.

Their guides led them down the twisting track that followed the valley, which had nearly blinded Suleiman earlier that day. It didn't seem the same place. No longer did heat come reflecting in sickening waves from off the white, reflecting crystalline deposit; no longer was there a glare so bright that they had felt it through the folds of their eye bandages.

Now they were passing through a shadowy land of vague whiteness that was like a scene set in snow. The night wind was warm, but not now unpleasantly so. And there was a calmness, a quietness that spoke of nearby sleep . . .

Tex's thoughts shied away from the depths of that possible sleep. His eyes probed the gathering gloom, and his brain raced madly in an effort to conjure up some plan of escape. But what could they do, for all they were mounted and their escorts were afoot? For their horses were securely held, and to every rider were at least two riflemen.

Nicky managed to get her horse up alongside his own. He heard her voice, plaintive and bewildered: 'Tex, I don't understand you. Why didn't we stay? We should have refused to go without poor Mahfra.'

They had followed him out of habit,

because he was their leader, when he had given the word to ride out into the night. He realised that if he had ordered defiance of those guns, they would have stood their ground and challenged death.

He could only whisper, in his agony: 'Oh, Nicky, don't ask me!' For even now he didn't want her to know she was going to be killed when the desert was reached.

His eyes looked into the shadows, looked up at the smooth white slopes that still caught light reflected from the dust-laden sky. And never an idea came to him that suggested a possibility of escape. Then he looked at Rube. Rube was watching him intently. When he saw that Rube's eyes were upon him, he nodded slightly. He didn't know what he intended to convey with that nod, but he knew that Rube was alert and he wanted him to act when he acted.

When he acted . . . When? He thought: 'The moment we come out of this damn valley, I'm gonna jump off my horse right on to that fellar with my Lebel!'

If he were lucky, he might wrest it from the Arab and might fight his way out of their grasp, taking Nicky and his comrades with him. But at the back of his mind was the thought that he'd be shot even while he was jumping from his saddle. They must surely be waiting for such a move.

Their horses plodded on, heads downwards, as is the way with Arab horses in the desert, however fresh they are. Their unshod hooves crunched softly into the flawless white salt, hardly making a sound. Five horses, four men and a girl mounted upon them, and a dozen or fifteen ragged Arabs marching on either side of them, like a guard of honour.

Suleiman had come with his comrades, but the leader of the Brotherhood was back in the cavern with the remainder of the men. Tex kept looking across at the big, gangling Arab in the skull cap and long ragged gown, but by now it was so dark that he couldn't see anything but pools of shadow on that hideous face.

They came at last on to ground that sloped hardly at all. It was grey now, from the treading of dirt off the desert. They were still within that white valley, however, though they knew they must be near to the end of it. Already Tex thought that he could smell the brush that lived so miraculously without water for months on end, and was aromatic after dark.

Within minutes now there would be the end for them and their plans. Already the Arabs leading their horses were hurrying, as if they wished to get this thing over before the light completely failed —

Minutes? Perhaps they had only seconds to live . . .

It was where the valley was at its narrowest. Now the night was so dark that already pale stars were beginning to show and grow in the grey-black of the sky. Everywhere were shadows, starkly black against the fading white slopes of the Valley-where-men-go-blind.

He was riding with his head forward, peering, trying to think ahead and plan. He passed a pocket of blackness and his horse shied and reared away. His head looked back into that shadow, and his eyes tried to see what had alarmed the horse.

There were shadows on either side of

them, and a bigger shadow ahead where a tongue of salt lay almost completely across the valley. His horse jumped sideways at the next patch of blackness, and its nervousness seemed to communicate itself to the other beasts, for they all became temperamental and unmanageable.

He heard the familiar yapping voice of his comrade from Brooklyn, surprised and uncertain: 'What'n Hades . . . Gid down, you ol' hoss. There ain't nuthin' to scare youse, so keep them feet outa the sky, see?'

That yapping voice saved their lives.

Startled, Tex saw a shape form out of the darkness, silhouetted against that spit of salt. A man's crouching form; a man holding something that could have been a rifle levelled.

His eyes, incredulous, travelled sideways. There was another crouching rifleman — another coming into shape as he sought to find them . . . another, another and yet another. Many of them, strung in line across their path.

And now he knew what had lurked in those shadows, startling their sensitive horses, knew who was back on the trail behind them now.

A raucous bellow shattered the quiet of that valley. *'Halte! Qui est-il?'*

It was a voice they knew. Not long ago he had been their *chef*, their sergeant-major in the Foreign Legion.

The Legion had arrived at the Valley-where-men-go-blind. Tex and his two deserter-comrades had fallen into the hands of the Legion again.

7

Old Comrades

'Ransconsi!' Tex heard the incredulous cry from Rube, his comrade. Ransconsi the Italian — the Bullfrog of the Pontine Marshes, as the cynics called him in the regiment. Heavy-jawed and blue-chinned, there were men who swore that each day he spent an hour before his mirror, practising forbidding expressions in the manner-Mussolini.

He was an arrogant, strutting man of, at times, savage disposition, but he was a man of courage, for all that.

Tex shouted: 'Don't shoot, *chef*!' And then, quickly, to the startled Arab escort — 'Hold your fire, Suleiman. You're outnumbered!'

Things happened within seconds at that. All at once the Arabs seemed to flit together, around the grim form of the tall Suleiman, as if prepared to sell their lives dearly at the entrance to their secret hideout in the salt cave. Rube and Elly took advantage of the release on their bridles and sent their horses rearing up around their leader, Tex. He caught the white shapes of Nicky in her blouse and 'brahim in his flowing burnouse and was reassured. They were all together, safe for the moment.

Ransconsi's voice came harshly to them. 'Don't try any tricks, any of you. I have many men with me, and at the first sign of treachery you will all die.'

With that he came marching forward, tough and cocky, ignoring any possible danger to himself. There was still some light, and Tex was able to see that familiar face under his kepi. Ransconsi's chin was jutting and his eyes were rimmed with white as they protruded in their effort to see who was on those horses.

'*Arabis*,' Tex heard in contempt. 'And — one, two, three — three of the Legion!' Ransconsi shouted imperatively: 'You, what is the meaning of this?'

Joe Ellighan was the nearest to him, and his voice began to yap, happily:

'There ain't no meanin', brother. We jus kinda like a lotta salt in our water, so we came here.'

Tex shoved his mount across, quickly. His brain was racing madly, filled with ideas. He wanted to stop Elly from speaking. A few incautious words and the guns would open up, and a lot of people might die who need not.

He found himself near to Suleiman, crouching back with his men. Suleiman's eyes seemed to shine up at him, as if luminous with hatred and fear.

Tex heard his curious Scottish accent — 'Many will die, even though we die — '

Tex called, gruffly: 'Don't start anything, brother!'

Then he was talking to Ransconsi, talking to save their lives.

He had Ransconsi by the hand, a familiarity that the *chef* was disposed to overlook because he had expected trouble, with the sound of their approach, and not this unexpected meeting and friendliness.

'Brother,' Tex was saying heartily, 'am I glad to see you! The hell, we thought we were never gonna get out of this goddamned desert!'

Rube was off his horse in a minute, quick-witted Rube picking up his cue. He was in among those silent legionnaires with their suspicious, pointing guns, shaking hands and slapping them on the back like a man so relieved to be among friends that his words were hardly coherent.

'You wouldn't know the miles we've tramped, tryin' to keep one jump ahead of Arabs. You wouldn't know what it's like, to be lost in this neck o' country. Boy, am I glad to see you!'

His comrades were glad to see him, too. They relaxed and melted, overjoyed to have found more allies instead of having a grim battle against an enemy who could only weaken them even if they weren't completely wiped out.

But Ransconsi was no fool. At once his voice rang out — 'Who are these Arabs?'

It stopped Rube's chattering tongue. It brought stillness to Joe Ellighan's yapping, excited mouth. Nicky came close up against Tex, as if she thought that this time her presence would help him in the answer he had to make. Sheik 'brahim sat his mount in silence, waiting for the answer that was to send the guns blazing.

Tex looked again into that face of this complex personality that was Suleiman. He knew that Arab rifles were pointing at him, that he would be the first to die if he brought death raining upon the Brotherhood.

But it wasn't fear that dictated his answer. It was something more than that, and he didn't know the full reason himself until he had spent the next days thinking on what he had said.

Almost in surprise he heard his own voice say: 'They are friends, *chef*. They have given us water and were sending us on our way.'

There was a gasp from Nicky. She didn't know the full truth, and now it was a good thing she hadn't known it. But plainly she had become worried and been made suspicious by the Brotherhood's conduct in the last hour.

'Friends — and they have water.' Ransconsi's voice was full of satisfaction. Tex understood then that water had become the nightmare of this band of wandering legionnaires.

'You need water?'

'*Parbleu*. Listen to the child.' The *chef* was in a mood of jocular exaggeration. 'He asks us, do we need water?'

There was the usual sycophantic murmur of approving laughter that will follow any sergeant-major's attempt at humour, no matter what army he is in.

Tex could sense the relaxing in the dark, as the legionnaires dropped their vigilance. They were among friends. The relief was enormous. For days they had never seen a man, almost, but what he was wanting to kill them. He heard the excited, delighted voices, the quick little laughs that spoke of a previous tension.

Suleiman was watching him, still suspicious because he and his men were surrounded and these accursed soldiers from Europe had many guns to their few.

Ransconsi the Italian exclaimed: 'Where is this water? Let us go to it for we are almost without ourselves.'

Tex felt the stiffening of Suleiman, and knew he was antagonistic to the idea. He found himself opposed to it also, for another reason. He had to stop the legionnaires from going up to that hiding-place of the Brotherhood, for he was certain of the result if they did try to enter the cavern.

The Brotherhood, in full force, would oppose the legionnaires. There would be fighting, death to one side or the other. And Mahfra was with the Brotherhood and might suffer in the fighting, for flying bullets do not discriminate.

There was another reason why they must not try to enter that cave . . .

He called: 'Suleiman — my good friend Suleiman — will return with your waterskins and bottles and fill them. For assuredly you will break your necks if you try to find your way up this valley now, in this darkness. Let us go out on to the desert and await the return of these Arabs.'

Tex's quick-wittedness saved the situation. He heard an exclamation of approval from Suleiman; heard him muttering an explanation to his brethren. Then skins were being handed across, along with a few *bidons*, the water bottles of the Legion.

Suleiman gave an order to his men and they were accepted.

Tex found a rifle being pushed into his hands in the darkness. Suleiman was putting his life in his, Tex's, hands.

He heard the soft Scottish accent: 'Why did you do that? Why save our lives when you know what we intended to do?'

Tex didn't answer, because he wasn't sure what the answer was himself. He felt better with the Lebel in his hand, and it saved awkward explanations if Ransconsi noticed their Lebels in possession of their Arab 'friends'.

He rode away out of the valley, wanting to get on to the open desert. The legionnaires came marching through the darkness after him. He realised that Nicky was riding on one side of him, Joe Ellighan on the other.

Joe's whispered voice reached his ears. 'What'n heck do we do now, Tex? We ain't gonna stay with the Legion, are we?'

And Rube's voice came across, disconcertingly loud: 'They haven't got hosses. When we're outa the valley, let's scram. They'll never catch us.'

Tex thought that one out, then shook his head, though they didn't see it because of the night. 'Nope. Do that an' Ransconsi's suspicions will be aroused. Sure as hell he'll want to go an' find out what's up that valley. Then there'll be trouble — fightin'. If they win they'll find Sturmer, an' then we'll have lost him agen.'

'You're plannin' on getting' hold of Sturmer agen?'

'That's still the plan.' Tex's voice was grim. The more he was thwarted, the more determined he became to accomplish his mission, to take ex-General Herman Sturmer back for trial for his war crimes. He didn't want a situation whereby he lost sight of the man again, and had to start searching the desert for him. He mightn't be able to recapture him again.

His voice growled out a quick explanation. 'We've got to lead Ransconsi away from this valley of salt. We know Sturmer's here, an' I figger on comin' back for him when we've dodged the *chef*. But we've got to stick close to

Ransconsi for a few hours, until he is well out of the district. There's Mahfra, too; we've got to try to help her.'

Rube saw the idea and became suddenly enthusiastic. 'Sure, sure,' they heard him say. 'You've got the idea, Tex. That's what we'll do. Ransconsi doesn't suspect we're on pump.'

'Nope. He won't know we're deserters. Not if we stick to our tale that we were trying to break through the Arab lines like they were.'

They went out on to the broad, level desert. Ransconsi ordered fires to be lit from the brush that was plentiful hereabouts, and when they blazed, the last grains of some precious coffee were boiled up.

Everyone sat round the fires, the red glow illuminating their weary, dust-grey faces. But it was a cheerful gathering. They were among friendly Arabs. They could even light fires in safety. And there was water coming to them. There was much laughter and talking, and the unaccustomed coffee seemed to affect them like alcohol.

Men came to shake the three legionnaires by the hand. Old comrades from the fort at El Kwatra that had been destroyed in a recent Arab uprising.

They told their stories, of how they had escaped with their lives, that night that the Legion post was assaulted. The darkness that had helped the Arabs to make their surprise attack, had also helped them to escape.

'That *chef*,' said one of them. 'He is a pig and the son of a diseased camel, but he is a man of courage. He gathered us together, we few who had escaped, and then we fought our way through the Arab forces, taking precious water and food from our slain enemies until we were well away. For days since then we have been trying to get round the Arab armies, to rejoin our comrades in the north and east. We have been lucky. A few times we encountered small bands of horsemen riding to rejoin the main Arab army.'

The speaker shrugged. 'We attacked them — either that or they attacked us. We won, though we lost two of our comrades in one little skirmish.'

Tex looked at the speaker, a stocky, pleasant little German-Swiss who had joined the Legion because he was too good-natured. He had spent a lot of money on his friends, to give them some pleasure in life, because they were mostly poor and had less than their share of good things. Unfortunately the money hadn't been his, and his employer had set the police after him. The Legion had opened up her arms and given him shelter, though he was of the freely expressed opinion that a Swiss jail would have been an easier way of life.

'You have suffered,' agreed Tex sympathetically. 'But so have we. Now we are all together, *mon enfant*, assuredly it will be better for us.'

He wanted to ask the legionnaire how they had come to be entering the Valley-where-men-go-blind in search of water, for not even nomads like 'brahim knew that it existed within its white folds. But his eyes were counting the horses, revealed by the dancing firelight. His brow puckered . . .

He heard Rube ending a fanciful

account of their adventures since the fall of Fortress El Kwatra, Rube forgetting to say that they had gone 'on pump' a few hours before the attack on the place. Then Rube asked the question that was in his mind.

'What're you doing here? What brought you to this white hell?'

. . . four horses only. Tex counted again. There had been five horses when they rode out of the valley.

He looked round the firelight, but he didn't see three men who sat back in the shadows, but whose eyes never left his face.

He heard the reply to Rube's question, from an Alsatian who was known as The Mouth — a man who could never keep his tongue still.

They had been wandering in the desert, almost out of water, marching by night and resting by day. The previous night they had heard a horse whinny; they had kept on, not knowing how big was the Arab force that was seemingly encamped some-where in the darkness.

With the heat of the sun, they had

rested, keeping watch against surprise. When they resumed their march, late that afternoon, they had come across the tracks of a small party of horsemen, and they had followed, hoping the trail would lead to water.

'And it did, *ma foi*!' exclaimed the garrulous Alsatian. '*Voila*, and here it comes!' For at that moment Suleiman and his ragged followers came within view of the firelight bearing the heavy water-skins on their backs.

Rube and Joe Ellighan were grinning at each other. But they didn't say whose horse it was that had whinnied, whose tracks they were that had led the party into the Valley-where-men-go-blind. The legionnaires didn't need to know that.

Four horses, Tex thought again, as Suleiman began to step across the feet of the sprawling legionnaires towards him. Rube, Joe, Nicky — himself. All there.

'brahim!

The sheik must have stolen silently away on his horse in the confusion when they left the valley.

Suleiman came across to the fire, bent

and whispered: 'Your tongue will be silent?'

'About you and the valley?' Suleiman's eyes were intent, watching his face.

'About the Brotherhood.'

'The Legion will not be told,' Tex said.

Suleiman sighed with relief and straightened. He looked immensely tall, standing above Tex in his tattered gown.

'Our lives are in your hands,' he heard the Arab say. 'You know the secret of the Valley-where-men-go-blind. Think well before you betray it, for the Brotherhood of Tormented Men live only to help their oppressed fellows in the Arab world.'

Tex nodded slowly. He said: 'I have given thought to it, and I will see that none of my friends here speak.'

Suleiman, the Arab who had learned his democracy in a Northern university, bent for a second and his big, rough hand touched Tex's shoulder lightly, in a gesture of friendship and gratitude.

'It was not necessary . . . what we planned,' Tex heard him say. 'It seems you too are of the Tormented Men. Our secret is safe in your keeping.'

But Tex was thinking of that missing horse — and 'brahim.

The secret of the Brotherhood was in jeopardy now that 'brahim, impulsive and ardent, rode the desert beyond his, Tex's, control.

He thought: 'Trouble's gonna come after this. Plenty trouble.'

8

They're Assassins!

As Suleiman was about to stride away
into a darkness that seemed the darker
because of this leaping firelight, Tex
caught his *galabier* and held him.

'Mahfra?' he asked softly.

'No harm will come to her.'

'You kept her back to save her life. You
want her, and you weren't prepared to let
her die with us.' Tex had guessed that
before.

'Sturmer?' That was his next question.

'Keep our secret, be our friend, and
you can have him when we've finished
with him. Come for him; you will be safe
this time — if your tongue hasn't spoken.'
Suleiman spoke in gratitude. This Westerner, whose life they had been about to
take, had it in his power to destroy them,
yet for his own purposes he had not
betrayed them. Suleiman knew then that

the Texan was in sympathy with a Brotherhood that had suffered without justice to their sufferings.

'If I had only known,' Suleiman repeated, and Tex caught the flashing smile in the firelight. Then Suleiman went away with his men, into the valley and beyond their sight.

Sentries were posted. Sleep came upon them, the sleep that comes when life is assured by an abundance of water and promise of friendliness. They slept at ease, the *chef*, nineteen legionnaires of the French Foreign Legion, and one American girl.

But three men slept apart in the shadows, beyond sight of the newcomers. Before they stretched themselves on the soft, warm sand, however, they held converse, and it was swift and urgent.

'Those accursed Americanos — '

'Our necks are no longer safe. They know so much — about Fort El Kwatra . . . '

They looked at each other, bitter-eyed men who were lucky to have heads upon their shoulders, and who had thought their infamy had been lost in death. One spoke, a man who had taken heads before.

He said: 'They must die before they see our faces. Or we must escape again. Tomorrow, perhaps . . . '

The party moved an hour before dawn. Tex heard the sergeant-major's rough voice getting men up on to their feet. The laggards he assisted with his boot. Ransconsi was brave, but he was brutal.

They set off north and east, towards the French cities along the Gulf de Gabes, in the Mediterranean. When light came, however, they were still well within sight of that massive white mountain that had nearly been the death of Tex and his companions.

Looking back, the American saw tiny specks toiling in their wake. His eyes narrowed thoughtfully. Distance made it difficult to count them, but he thought there must have been a dozen or twenty in that tiny, following band.

The Brotherhood, of course. He thought: 'What are they up to? Where are they going?'

They'd come into this desert on some hazardous mission, he knew, and now he wondered if they were about to set off to accomplish their unknown task. He shrugged. He still couldn't make up his mind about the Brotherhood, still wasn't sure he had done the right thing in pretending they were his friends. Then he thought: 'Sure, I did right.' Suleiman said no harm would come to Mahfra, and ex-General Sturmer was his for the collecting. Sure his tactics had been right — now the Brotherhood were in his power, and friends.

The thought came jumping into his mind that perhaps the party behind them wasn't setting off on some secret mission, but might be dogging the legionnaires' footsteps with a view to silencing Tex and his comrades. He shrugged. It was possible, but somehow he didn't think so.

Before noon they halted for a four-hour rest during the worst heat of the day. They lay down gasping, because this day was as torrid as any they had known. When they'd been down for three hours, a sentry came stumbling from off a small hillock to report camel riders on the horizon.

They all rose and went up to see this new threat. About a dozen Arabs had come across their tracks. Now they were sitting their ugly, long-legged mounts about a quarter of a mile away and watching them.

While they watched, three of their number spurred off towards the north-west, passing them in a cloud of dust that rose almost up to the saddlecloths. They were within rifle range when they passed, but Ransconsi ordered his men not to fire. Ammunition was valuable, and there was no sense in antagonising people, was his argument.

The legionnaires watched gloomily, first at the Arabs watching from the hill to the south of them, then at the dust cloud that told of the stiff-legged trotting of the long-limbed camels.

Tex spoke their thoughts. 'Racin' camels.' That put these camel-riders down as scouts from a war-party. Those fast-running camels would be off with news of their presence to the main force.

The thought was depressing.

Ransconsi went into a black rage. '*Mon dieu!*' he kept saying. 'Must this go on always? What have we done to deserve this bad luck?' His black, Neapolitan eyes regarded the three Americans with sudden disfavour. 'Perhaps you *miserables* have brought a curse upon us.'

He was in a mood to find fault with his followers, and he enlarged upon the theme for some time. Then he came out with a sentence that surprised the listening Americans. 'Six new recruits, all in one day. I thought our troubles were over. Now it seems they are just beginning.'

Six? Tex wondered who the other three could be, and where they had come from in the desert, but he forebore to ask because Ransconsi plainly was in no mood to answer questions.

Then came a blow to Tex's plans. During the long afternoon break, his two American comrades and Nicky had come to him to discuss the situation. Lying there, apart from their fellows — watched all the time, though they didn't know it

— they talked of the break for freedom.

'Tonight,' they had agreed. 'Our horses will be pretty fresh because they're going at walking pace all day. The moment it is dark enough, we'll just ride away from the legionnaires They won't come after us, because we'll be heading south and that's the wrong way for marching legionnaires. We'll go back to the cave in the salt hill.'

'And then?' Nicky had questioned anxiously.

'Then,' said Tex, 'you'll stay out on the desert an' I'll go up to the cave when the sun's down an' the valley doesn't blind me with its light.'

'You're not afraid?'

Tex shrugged. This wasn't a time to bother about fear. 'I reckon Suleiman meant it when he said next time we met we'd be among friends.'

Nicky tried to figure that one out. She wrinkled her nose and looked with distaste at the sweating, snoring manhood sprawled around her.

'I still don't know whether that Brotherhood was friendly towards us or not. They certainly did us no harm, but

— well, all the time I had a feeling they didn't intend to do us any good.'

'You don't know!' whispered Tex to himself, and he didn't tell his companions the truth of that situation. They'd think him screwy if he did. He wondered yet again if he had been wrong in his head. Going out to be killed, then calling his cold-blooded captors 'friends'.

It was all involved, yet Tex felt that he had handled things satisfactorily. But though he didn't tell them what the Brotherhood had intended to do once they got them out on the desert, he was yet incapable of resisting an urge to shock them.

He said, dryly: 'I figger you don't know what the Brotherhood are, do you?'

Then he told them, before they could make guesses.

'They're — assassins!'

Once the camel riders came into view, they never saw that toiling band of Brotherhood again. It was as if they kept out of sight because of that armed party, sitting so silently there on the humps of their camels, sinister in their white, hooded burnouses.

Before their siesta was quite finished, Ransconsi kicked them to their feet again. Now, with those silent watchers to prey on their nerves, he was becoming more out of temper, was more brutal in his actions.

When Tex went to get his horse, he found the sergeant-major mounting. Tex halted, his kepi flapping around his ears as a heat-laden wind stirred along the desert and sent dust devils spiralling. His eyes glinted as he looked up into that bullfrog face.

Ransconsi sneered down at him. 'It is not fitting that a legionnaire should ride when his superior has to walk. You are to be congratulated on providing such a superb beast for your *chef*. Rejoin your comrades, and feel proud that you have pleased me.'

Tex watched him ride away, and his fists clenched. Then he saw a sergeant and a corporal take their cue from the *chef*. Rube and Joe Ellighan were forced to dismount so that their 'superiors' could ride instead of walking. Joe lost his customary good humour and wanted to walk in with his fists flying, but Rube and Tex held him back. In the Legion a legionnaire was nothing, and even a corporal was a god whose will must not be crossed.

Their eyes watched after their horses sombrely. Tex growled: 'The hell, this is gonna bust up our plans.'

He didn't realise that with the presence of those hooded camel riders, everyone's plans were upset.

Ransconsi led the way, riding alongside Nicky. He was gallant, but his manner was offensive, too. If a corporal was a god in the Legion, what, then, was a sergeant-major with over twenty years' service?

Ransconsi always took what he wanted. Now he was deciding that he wanted this American girl, and he couldn't think of any reason why he shouldn't have her. Wasn't he Ransconsi, the *chef*? Then who was there among this scum to say nay to his desires?

He never thought that Nicky might have ideas opposed to his own; after all, he was a fine figure of a man, wasn't he? And didn't the women in the cafés at Sidi-bel-Illah all smile at him and want his favours?

He told Nicky this, proudly. Nicky said: 'Brother, your technique's crude. That won't get you any place.' But the Bullfrog of the Pontine Marshes didn't understand Americanese.

Rube growled: 'You wanna watch that fat frog, Tex. He's got ideas about Nicky.'

Tex just answered: 'She c'n take care of herself.' But he didn't feel sure. Ransconsi, like most undeserving bullies, had his followers. What he said went with this party.

Tex sighed and wished he had a revolver. Suleiman had returned them their rifles, but not the revolver he had been carrying. And Tex liked a six-shooter. There were times when a revolver was a handier weapon than a rifle.

They rode and marched while the sun came down towards the eastern horizon. They all knew the tactics that Ransconsi would employ to throw off pursuit. They would keep marching during the night, changing their direction so as to elude the

166

scouts on their camels. That might give them a breathing space before their tracks were followed with daylight.

But the moon rose early that night, less than half an hour after sunset. True it was a starved and miserable little moon, but on that near-white desert its illumination was considerable.

When they looked behind, the camel riders were watching them from the swaying saddles on their camels. Unless clouds came to obscure the feeble moon, they weren't going to dodge the Arabs in the night.

Shortly after midnight, Ransconsi gave it up. There wasn't a sign of a cloud in the sky — and those camel riders were riding parallel with them, On either side of them in the desert, so that now the legionnaires couldn't branch off unexpectedly without running into their foes.

Ransconsi got down from Tex's horse, swearing savagely, unmindful of the presence of the American girl. The accursed Arab swine couldn't be shaken off, he was declaring. Very well, they would rest during the night and conserve their strength, and tomorrow they would set ambushes and when the Arabs were trapped they would kill them all and their camels, too.

Those were further plans that weren't to mature. Just before dawn, a sentry woke Ransconsi to say that he had heard firing in the distance. The *chef* listened, but though the boy legionnaire declared that he could occasionally hear rifle fire, Ransconsi decided he was imagining it. He gave the order to continue the march.

When the sun came up the first thing they saw was the band of camel scouts, scattered in a big moving circle around them. The second, a dust cloud to the north and west of them.

That brought them to a halt, and they stood and peered across the undulating desert, trying to understand the meaning of that long column of dust that hung so motionless in the still morning air.

'That's an army on the move,' growled the legionnaires, one to the other. They watched it uneasily. Clearly it denoted the passage of a large body of men, but who they were they couldn't tell.

Ransconsi gave the order to get down off the skyline. If these were Arabs, then they were in sufficient force to wipe out the legionnaires without overmuch difficulty. They got down behind a long, wind-rippled dune, their faces grim as they watched that billowing cloud. They were too far away to distinguish anyone within it, but after a while it became apparent that it was moving across the line of their flight to the north of them.

Then a legionnaire shouted and began to curse. Everyone rose to look at him. He was a squat-looking bundle of ragged blue uniform up on the ridge. He was swearing ferociously, his hand pointing towards the west.

When they crawled up to him, they saw four of the camel riders loping off towards that hanging cloud of dust that covered a small army. Immediately Ransconsi and most of the other men added their curses to the first man's.

'God in heaven,' roared the *chef*, 'those dogs have gone to tell their rabble army that we are here!'

'*Les Arabis*,' the word went down the

line at that. 'The *chef* says they're Arabs.'

Some of the men rose immediately, preparing instinctively for flight, but Ransconsi shouted them down. There was no safety in flight, he told them, his heavy Italian face grim. What good would it do to tire themselves, and then for certain be overtaken by mounted Arabs? No, he ordered, they would dig themselves in on this ridge and defend it to the last bullet. This was as good a place as any to make a stand; this patch of desert would serve as a grave as well as another a couple of miles off.

He was a man of high courage, though even his thoughts were brutal. He called for someone to take the horses into a hollow where they would be protected from flying bullets. Three legionnaires took them and led them away. Then the *chef* placed his men on surrounding ridges, and they all lay down to watch the approach of the camel scouts to that distant dust cloud.

Tex and his comrades got down alongside Nicky. The Texan gave her a long drink from a *bidon*, because he thought she would need it in this time of peril.

She smiled at him, but he could see the shadow of fear lurking in those blue eyes. He asked, gently: 'Scared?'

Nicky nodded. 'I've been scared for days, so this isn't unusual.' She was making a brave attempt to be light-hearted.

He put his arm round her. 'Don't lose heart,' he whispered. 'Just think, we've been in some tight spots, but — well, we got out of them, I reckon. We'll get out of this, too.'

They lay there on their stomachs, watching those receding specks that were long-legged camels and huddled riders. The sun blazed down upon them, making them feel sick, and the air danced over the grey-yellow sand of the desert, so that nothing remained still for a second and all the world was distorted.

There was silence over the grim but discouraged legionnaires. They had gone through so much, had survived so many perils; they had begun to think their troubles were over, almost — and now

171

they were faced with the greatest threat.

Tex looked round at them, trying to read their thoughts, and hoping they wouldn't be able to read his. His eye searched across the empty hollow to where Ransconsi watched from the highest point. He was an ugly man, made uglier by the blue stubble of days, but he seemed dauntless in the face of peril. That was why the men never disputed his leadership, in spite of his brutality and sarcasm. They knew the *chef* to be their natural leader, and would follow him blindly.

Tex's eyes came slowly back. He saw trampled hoofmarks . . .

An uneasy little question began to hammer in his brain but for the moment it was obscured by other interests and it didn't emerge till later.

Nicky was speaking. 'It doesn't seem possible I'll ever see New York again, Tex.'

He thought she was cracking under the strain. He pulled her soft body gently towards him, and without quite realising what he was doing, kissed her on the cheek.

She flashed a smile at him. 'I've been

waiting for you to do that for a long time, you long-legged Texan. You're pretty slow, aren't you?'

Then she cuddled up to him, just for a moment, until that blazing sunshine drove them apart. 'I was going to say, Tex, I don't suppose we'll get out of this jam alive. This looks the worst of our ordeals, doesn't it? But I want you to know that — that I've met in you the finest man I've ever known.' Her eyes were shining, tears rising quickly as she looked at him.

He said: 'This is a fine time to tell a fellar that. You say all that agen in a coupla days' time when we're marchin' into some place where you'll be safe.'

She looked at him, wonderingly. 'Don't you ever lose courage, Tex?'

'Often. Too often.'

Her blonde head shook. 'I don't believe you. I don't think you've ever lost heart in your life.'

Those camel riders weren't going any nearer to that cloud now. They were circling, coming together. And that little question for some reason began to resurrect itself in Tex's mind. But he wanted to talk to Nicky; this conversation was bitter-sweet, but he wanted it to go on.

'Only a few hours ago I was so dead scared I couldn't think,' he told her, watching those camel riders. Then it was that he told her what fate had been intended for them by Suleiman and the Brotherhood when they led them along the Valley-where-men-go-blind.

'Ransconsi doesn't know it, but he figured in the rôle of angel of deliverance that night,' he ended. 'These legionnaires, springin' out of nowhere so unexpectedly, put an end to Suleiman's plans and saved our lives.'

Nicky had lain there, her head cradled on the soft sand, listening aghast to his story. She whispered: 'My god, Tex, I felt there was something wrong — I was uneasy all the time — but I never thought a man could be as treacherous as all that. And we saved Suleiman's life!'

Tex's eyes narrowed in perplexity. Those camel men were riding back towards their comrades who still kept watch on Ransconsi's party. He couldn't understand it. They had never approached that dust cloud by more than a half-mile.

He found himself defending Suleiman. 'Unless you've lived a life like Suleiman's, you'll never understand him. He's not a man any more; he's a walking mission.'

'Didn't you say, back there yesterday, that he and his brethren were — assassins?'

'I wasn't kiddin'. That's my guess. These Tormented Men have suffered so much that they've ganged together to wage war upon their oppressors. An' there's plenty, here in the Arab countries,' he said grimly.

He looked at that soft, almost delicate woman's face so close to his, so different from the coarse, bearded faces around him.

'You've lived long enough in North Africa to know somethin' of what I'm talkin' about.' She nodded. He gestured, finding words difficult to say. 'The misery, the squalor, the disease and hunger — they torment people more than the lash and burnin' irons, though there's plenty enough of that, by what I'm told. These countries are rotten.' His voice was suddenly savage. 'God, how I hate 'em. And it's men who are responsible for all this torment, a few greedy men who hold back progress and make millions suffer just so they can live better than the rest.'

Those camel men were coming in fast now, but that dust cloud hadn't deflected from its course and if anything it was receding to the north. Ransconsi was standing, talking animatedly to his sergeant.

Nicky said: 'I know what you mean, Tex. And the rotten, power-mad politicians are the worst of the lot.'

'Yeah, they're the worst.' Ransconsi was running down into that trampled, empty hollow, his heavy face a picture of conflicting emotions.

Nicky was saying: 'I don't understand you, all the same, Tex; I mean, treating Suleiman like a friend when he was prepared to kill you.'

'I don't understand myself.' Tex squinted back to where hooded camel men watched them from a high mound to the south. Their fellows were speeding in from that receding dust-cloud to the north of them.

The legionnaires everywhere around him were relaxing as the threat appeared to be disappearing.

'They had Mahfra a prisoner, an' Sturmer. I had some thoughts of preventin' fightin'. so that the gal wouldn't get hurt. I knew, too, that if it came to a fight both sides would suffer an' no one would gain any benefit from it. But there was another reason that kept me quiet about Suleiman.'

'Yes?'

Tex began to get to his feet. 'I kinda like the fellar, an' I feel — well, sympathetic towards him an' his aims.'

'Assassins though they are?'

'I don't know that for certain. It's a guess. I don't think I approve of assassination, but I approve less of all this mostly-unnecessary misery in the Arab world. Maybe sometimes it's no bad thing for a tyrant to be struck down. Maybe these Tormented Men are instruments of justice.'

Ransconsi was bellowing up at them: 'Fools that we are! That dust cloud comes from the tramping feet of legionnaires, not from Arab horsemen!'

That startled them. Perhaps some looked incredulous, for Ransconsi's furious, frustrated voice at once shouted an explanation.

'Would those dogs of camel men have kept away from that column if they had been of their own kind? But they didn't go in and speak to them, and I say it is because that column consists of soldiers of France and not of our Arab enemies. Now let us ride after that marching army, for when we reach it, we shall be safe!'

There were glad cries from the men, and even Nicky clasped Tex's arm exultantly. But Tex had suddenly found the answer to that hammering little question that had persisted these last minutes in his mind.

Ransconsi shouted: '*Mon sergent*, you and three men will take the horses and ride after that column. You will tell them of our presence, and beg that they will wait for us to catch up with them.'

He was a brute, but he did not take this opportunity of riding towards safety himself; instead he elected to stay with his little force, and gave the horse he had been riding to others.

'You will be able to outdistance those camels, though they are of a racing breed,' Ransconsi was saying, and then he realised how still and quiet and suddenly hopeless were the men all around him. They were looking at him, looking almost pityingly; for now he was the only man among them in ignorance.

Tex spoke, revealing the truth. 'No one can ride out after that column, my sergeant-major. And why? Because someone has stolen those horses!'

9

La Femme!

Now that they looked for them they could see their precious horses. One was running riderless, a mile to their south, pursued by two of the camel scouts. The other three were being ridden hard towards the east — so hard that they were not being pursued by others of the camel force.

Ransconsi screamed with rage, his face going black with anger inside him. His curses were fluent and expressive, and came from more languages than his native Italian.

'God's blood,' he raved. 'What sons of pigs have done this to us? Who was there among us who could betray us in order to save their own worthless skins?'

The sergeant-major was half-crazy with savage fury. All this time they had been lying there, letting friends and allies begin to march steadily away from them. Now, by treachery, they had lost the beasts that could have taken a message through, asking for succour.

Hastily there was a count among the men, a swift identification of those that remained. Then voices began to tell of the traitors who had been in their midst.

'*Mon chef*, those *canaille* are the three whom we rescued from the desert only two days ago . . . '

'They are Mervin Petrie . . . '

'The Bulgar of the rotten teeth . . . '

' . . . and La Femme.'

Rube's eyes almost shot from his head. Incredulously he looked at his comrades. Joe Ellighan's flat, battered features hung slackly open, staggered at the news. Then Tex, Nicky and the two legionnaires looked at each other — looked and could say nothing.

For Mervin Petrie, who had been assistant to the executioner at Marseilles; the Bulgar, who was a bully and a worthless scoundrel at heart; and La Femme — dainty, girl-like, but the rottenest villain in the whole French

Foreign Legion — these men had risen from the dead. Tex and his comrades could have sworn they had died out in the hills on the Libyan border.

Now they had suddenly reappeared, and in a typical act of treachery had put their comrades in a position of deadly danger again.

Ransconsi was a man of sound sense. He recovered and roared: 'Now that we know, forget about those *poumpists* until later. Now let us try to save our lives. *En avant, marche!*'

He plunged over the ridge, striding through the soft sand in the beginnings of a race after that column that offered so much in the way of safety. His men were after him instantly. They had to catch up with that receding column if they were to survive the dangers of this desert; for there must come a time when those camel scouts brought bands of Arabs down to attack them.

Tex took Nicky under the arm and helped her along. This was going to be hard enough for the men, but heaven knew the agonies it would bring to a girl.

She smiled up at him. 'Don't worry about me, Tex. I'll keep up with you.' He kept his hand under her arm, all the same. She'd never made a forced march across a desert and he had.

The sun rose higher and their shadows shortened. The sweat ran down their faces as they entered upon that forced march; the dust rose in clouds beneath their quickly-trudging feet, so that it mixed with the sweat and formed a grey, caking mass that masked them from their hair down to their tunic collars.

Hour after hour they tramped, led by the resolute, determined sergeant-major. He goaded them on with jeers and contemptuous curses; his words inflamed them, yet he kept the men moving.

But for a long time it seemed that they made no progress; in time it dawned upon the men that this still-unseen column of soldiery was also indulging in a forced march, and it made them uneasy.

By noon they were ready to drop, and still they hadn't seemingly gained a yard upon that slowly-rising cloud of dust to the north of them. And as they tramped through the yielding hot sand, the camel scouts kept pace with them on either flank, and it seemed to the thirsty, weary legionnaires that there was derision in their manner, as if they were sure this tiny party of legionnaires would never join the more powerful force.

'Soon,' thought Tex, 'those other scouts will be returning with reinforcements to attack us.'

If the attacking Arabs were strong enough, they could wipe out the sergeant-major's party within eyesight of that column that could mean their salvation. It wasn't a pleasant thought.

Tough, broad-shouldered ex-pugilist Joe Ellighan from Brooklyn had come up and taken Nicky's other arm. They marched together, lean, lanky Tex, and the squatter boxer.

Nicky protested. She could keep up with them, she declared. They'd got to stop regarding her as a weakling — wasn't she a woman who held down one of the toughest jobs on earth, foreign correspondent to an American newspaper?

Tex said, gently: 'You're up agen

another brand of toughness, honey. You'll need us before long, you see if you don't.'

She did. As the miles passed she grew heavier on their arms, but all the same she never gave in. If she had, they could never have kept up with their comrades, for the pace was fierce and relentless, the pace of one of the world's greatest marching forces, the French Foreign Legion.

At noon, when they were finally walking in their own shadows, the men had had enough, however. They began to beg for a halt, for a drink, for a rest — for anything except this mad rush across a desert that was never intended for marching feet.

Ransconsi wouldn't let up, however. He drove them on, calling them weaklings and old women who had lost the strength of their legs.

Then a weary band of legionnaires began to take an interest in a phenomenon ahead of them.

That dust cloud was slowly disappearing. For a few seconds as they saw it settle, men began to panic, thinking they were being left behind in the race. Then came an exultant shout from Ransconsi — 'See my children, the race is ours! See, they are settling down for the afternoon halt while the sun is at its hottest.'

It was true. Their eager straining eyes saw the dust cloud blow away as the tramping feet became still. More they saw a dull show of blueness, like an ink blot on the desert and realised they must have been gaining steadily during all the time they had marched along.

He was a good sergeant-major — good in the understanding of how to get the best out of marching men. He immediately called a halt for fifteen minutes so that they could drink and ease the weakness out of their legs. He told them to drink a lot, too, for water would be no use to them if they lost this race, and it weighed heavily on them, and they reckoned, anyway, there would be ample supplies if they caught up with the column.

They rested, lying on their backs and watching that distant, motionless stain of blueness with eyes that were fever-bright with anxiety. If they were in luck, those distant troops would rest for a full four hours, and in four hours they would be up to them.

Tex found himself next to the garrulous Alsatian. Even this situation could not still the tongue of the fellow, and he talked all the time. So after a while Tex began to ask him about the three legionnaires who had stolen the horses, which could so easily have brought relief to Ransconsi's little force.

'We found them in the desert.' The Alsatian was delighted to have a willing audience. 'They were tramping, near dead with thirst. When they saw us, the Bulgar began to weep with joy, for they had given themselves up for dead.'

'But not La Femme,' said Tex gently.

'Not La Femme,' agreed the Alsatian. 'La Femme has the softness of a woman facially, but his heart is hard. He is an evil one, that La Femme.'

The three legionnaires, wanderers over the face of the desert since the attack on Fortress El Kwatra — that was their story, anyway, and Tex did nothing to correct it — had told a tale of a fight with Arabs.

'The Arabs had got them trapped within the confines of a rocky canyon back in the mountains on the Libyan border.' The Alsatian found energy enough to wave to the south of them. 'It seemed that death was sure to come to them, when a miracle happened.

'It seems that on a rocky shelf to the side of the trail, between the Arabs and our friends Petrie, the Bulgar, and La Femme, was a number of horses left by some other riders. With all the firing — or perhaps maddened by thirst — some hours later they stampeded and came careering up the canyon. Petrie and his friends saw this heaven-sent opportunity to escape, and took advantage of it. As the horses came thundering by, they flung themselves on to their backs and were away before the attacking Arabs knew what was happening.'

Rube had one eye open. It was blue and highly sardonic. It looked at Tex and said without words: 'We know the truth of this story better than this talkative

188

Alsatian, don't we?'

They did. Those horses that had come running off the shelf had been theirs — Tex's, Rube's, Joe's and Nicky's. Tex and his friends had been trapped in that narrow gorge by La Femme and his merciless companions, who wanted to wipe out the sole witnesses to their infamy, for they had betrayed Fort El Kwatra to the Arab enemy.

But Tex and his friends had turned the tables on them — and left La Femme and cronies horseless and opposed to those savage hunters of Foreign Legion deserters, *les partizans*. That was why Tex had been so sure that the renegades were dead; rarely did a deserter escape from the dreaded headhunters once they had sighted a *poumpist* (deserter).

'What happened to their horses?' — Rube.

'They were without water; if there had been waterskins on those horses, they must have been flung off in the stampede. So one by one they had to kill those beasts, for the liquid that was with their meat. As you know, horseflesh is not quenching, and when we met them they had slaughtered their last horse and were still gripped by a thirst that was intolerable.' He shrugged. 'And we had little enough water in all conscience, until we met you, *mon camarade.*'

It explained a lot. Tex thought: 'They were in this party all the time, and I never knew it. They must have kept away from us, deliberately. And at the first opportunity they deserted again.'

Ransconsi was shouting them to their feet once more. Tex lingered with his thoughts. 'We alone know they treacherously betrayed Fort El Kwatra to the enemy in return for a promise of safe conduct through Arab country to a seaport whence they could find a boat across to Europe. Only, with the outbreak of Arab warfare, the French had thrown armies across the coast area, and La Femme and friends, had been forced to turn back into the desert.

La Femme, Mervyn Petrie and the Bulgar had run away now because they had feared exposure and death if Tex and his friends had recognised them . . .

That blue stain upon the distant desert hadn't moved. They stirred their creaking, stiffening limbs into a further frenzy of activity, hastening with all speed towards those distant soldiers.

For an hour they ploughed grimly on, though the heat from that reflecting desert seemed to suffocate them, and every stride became an agony that was only surpassed by the next one. Each time they topped a rise and were able to look towards the northern horizon their eyes tried to measure progress. In time they could see that they were in fact lessening the gap, but it seemed to be accomplished impossibly slowly.

And always as they staggered along, those easy-riding camel scouts kept pace with them, seeming to jeer at their clumsy progress as their brown faces watched contemptuously from under the hoods of their white burnouses.

After an hour and a half, Ransconsi was obliged to give them another rest. Obliged — because the men took it. They'd followed their energetic, tireless leader up a slope that was a mountain of shifting sand. It had been a desperate fight to get each foot out of the treacherous, holding grains, so that when they reached the summit they just lay down where they were.

Ransconsi lay on his side, too, but he shouted to them to get up and keep moving. Did they want that siesta to come to an end before they were sighted by their distant comrades? Did they want to struggle all this way, only to lie down now like helpless babes and let the column march off without them?

There were men who now answered tiredly that the column could rot in the desert for all they cared. Just now they must rest; and they stretched themselves and panted and groaned, and in the end Ransconsi the Italian Bullfrog had to yield to them.

He gave them another fifteen minutes. Nicky lay helpless on Tex's arm. Her face was white now, and he was alarmed. This desert was no place for a woman, and he thought: 'She'll never make it, not on her own two legs.'

Then grim resolve came into his mind.

She would reach the safety promised by those other legionnaires if he had to carry her the last five miles on his back!

. . . Ransconsi was calling. God in heaven, that wasn't fifteen minutes. That wasn't even fifteen seconds they protested. But they stirred, finding strength in their limbs that hadn't been there a quarter of an hour before.

Tex pulled the American girl on to her feet. Rube took Joe Ellighan's place this time. He pulled her arm across his neck; cracked: 'I've been wantin' to get my arm around you ever since we met, babe.'

She smiled, but was too weary to make an answer. Tex rapped back: 'She's my gal. You take liberties, brother, an' Ransconsi will be without a first-class machine-gunner.'

He was turning, getting into line with the other rising, cursing legionnaires, when he saw a man lift a rifle and fire. The rifle had seemed to point towards Ransconsi, and before the white smoke cleared, Tex thought for a moment that the sergeant-major had been fired upon.

He saw Ransconsi go spinning round in

alarm, then drop to the sand. But Ransconsi had got his revolver out and was firing down the slope.

Tex unceremoniously dropped Nicky, unslinging his own Lebel. He saw camel men racing towards them, thought: 'They figgered to catch us off guard.'

They'd come sneaking up behind a dune, breaking out into a charge when the legionnaires seemed pre-occupied with thoughts of starting the march again. That vigilant little legionnaire had spotted them in time however, and given his comrades chance to defend themselves.

Rifles snapped angrily, the sounds drifting in eddying waves across the desert. The camel men immediately pulled their mounts away and went headlong for cover. Their surprise attack had failed, and they weren't going to try any tricks with this well-armed little bunch of legionnaires.

Rube asked, perplexed: 'Now why did they do that?' They hadn't bothered to attack them before.

A veteran who had never risen higher than the rank of *Soldat 2ieme* class, answered sagely: 'The prey is escaping. This time when they saw us rise again to pursue our way, these *cochons* grew afraid that we would cheat them yet. Now they will harass us, to keep us from going too fast.'

And in another hour, even at their laborious pace they must surely be within close distance of their compatriots.

Then Ransconsi began to shout. He was in a fury again. Now he was pointing to the west. Low down on the horizon was another mighty moving cloud, and there was a swiftness about this dusty screen that told a story.

Without doubt these were mounted men, riding fast. And that meant, without much doubt, that they were Arabs.

Tex heard Rube groan: 'Those damn' camel men. They've found allies and are bringing them on to us.'

But Tex, seeing the size of that spreading cloud, shook his head. He was thinking: 'We're small stuff. They don't send an army that size to wipe out a handful of legionnaires.' He looked northwards. He thought: 'That's their target.' And now he knew why the legion troops resting to the north of them were indulging in forced marches.

They were a defeated force, on the run from this mighty Arab army.

He sighed but said nothing of his suspicions to his comrades. They thought they would be safe when they joined forces with their comrades. He shrugged. That Arab army looked big enough to upset anybody's ideas on safety, and they were cavalry, too.

They went down that long slope, rifles held ready, even Rube and Tex, with Nicky held upright between them. The camel men seemed to have wakened from sleep, and were now eager and vigilant, circling in a manner which spoke of the excitement that sight of that Arab army had brought them.

Suddenly they came in from the north, their ugly-headed camels covering the ground at a surprising pace. It was a frontal attack that was not sustained. As they rode in they let fly with their old muzzle-loaders, then wheeled swiftly into the desert beyond range of those deadly Lebels.

It hurt nobody, that swift attack, but it made the legionnaires halt for a minute or so until they saw the attack fade away, and that was probably all that the camel scouts wanted from the sortie — to delay the accursed infidels.

It also made the legionnaires proceed more cautiously. Now they had to halt before each ascent and send out their own scouts to make sure there were no camel men lurking below the horizon, waiting to surprise them. It was correct desert tactics, but it reduced the pace of the anxious legionnaires very considerably.

Now they looked at the sun and wished that it didn't descend so quickly. For when the greatest heat was taken from it, then the distant troops would rise from their painful siesta — and leave them behind.

It was this thought that kept the men cursing ferociously, and ready to use their rifles on any target. It made the Arab camel men cautious, but still they kept riding in, trying to slow down their pace.

Two camel men were shot and went

reeling away. Then one of the legionnaires had his kepi shot off — and part of his scalp went with it. But though he was hurt, the man went on. That was how they were trained in the Legion — to keep on in spite of scratches.

They struggled on now, out of sight of that still-distant column of French soldiery. They were crossing a basin in the sandy waste, a basin quite two miles wide. Just beyond it was the resting force that wore French blue. Two miles to go.

But though they could no longer see the Legion troops, all the time they were able to see that advancing Arab army, storming northwards along a ridge top, their hard-pressed horses sending the dust of the desert fifty feet into the air from their kicking hooves — a grey-yellow cloud that hung for the better part of half an hour, and so stayed as a train right back to the horizon, to mark the passage of the Arab Nationalists.

That basin was an inferno of heat. It was as if it collected the rays of the sun, fierce enough without any further assistance, and flung them from all angles on to the struggling, gasping band of men and one woman, dragging their way through a sand that held their feet and made every stride a struggle in itself.

Tex taking more and more of Nicky's weight on to his broad shoulder, kept looking at her. Always she smiled at him; her spirit was good if her strength was not up to that of these trained soldiers of the Legion.

'Can you make it, honey?' he asked once. That ride which promised at least temporary safety seemed as far off as ever. The dread that was in all their hearts was that eventually they might make it, only to find the Legion had marched off, disturbed by sight of the rapidly-approaching Arab army. But no one spoke of that terror; sufficient when it came . . .

'I'll make it,' she retorted. 'If you can hold out, Tex.'

For she knew that while there was strength in him, he would never go on without her.

Joe Ellighan was back on the other side of her, helping her along. He and Rube were taking it in turns to assist her, but Tex seemed inspired and tireless and wouldn't be relieved from her other side.

When they were right in the middle of the basin, all at once the camel-riders' attack on them flared into an all-out assault. It was as if they were in a rage and panic lest this enemy whom they had dogged for so long should escape them right at the last minute.

'*Hola!*' screamed Ransconsi, in the lead, suddenly, and went down into the sand.

10

Arab Avengers

Like a flight of avenging furies, the troop of camel scouts was hurtling in to the attack, riding in from all angles. Tex saw the swaying necks and the white, huddled figures on the high humps; he saw the plumes of smoke snatched away by the speed of their progress, and heard the muffled explosion of old muzzle-loaders directly afterwards.

He let Nicky drop into the soft sand, and knelt alongside her, his rifle springing to his shoulder and firing in the same movement. He aimed for the camels; that was a surer mark than those elusive targets high up on the swaying humps. He put a halt to a sharp attack to the west of them, snapping off rounds quicker than his yet-well-trained comrades.

Lead was screaming in upon them, sending them grovelling down into the sand. Ransconsi was shouting encouragement and calling abuse at the Arabs at the same time. Somehow some of the camel men got through, charging right in among them.

From their position on the sand, the camels looked tremendous, suddenly trampling right on top of them. They were frightened by the fighting, and made vicious with it. Tex saw ugly heads, hissing out a bubbling anger; saw long yellow teeth — and saw the mouths open as the heads struck, snakelike, at the legionnaires beneath their padded feet.

Tex was up immediately, swinging his rifle and battering back the attack, holding them away from the girl on the ground. Rube came jumping in, rifle firing until it was empty, and then standing alongside Tex and using his rifle as a club. Joe Ellighan staggered through to join them. He was bleeding from a cut over his eyes that had been caused by a flashing Arab sword.

There was a hectic moment of close-quarter fighting — the fierce-eyed, bearded Arabs shrieking their war cries from high upon the saddles of their mounts; the desperately striving legionnaires finding strength to hit back and even drive them back.

But Ransconsi's revolver turned the tide, eventually. As a sergeant-major he was issued with a revolver, though there were many in the Legion who said they were given to protect *chefs* against the soldiers they led, and were not primarily for use against France's enemies.

Now, at close quarters, it proved invaluable. It had stuck, after the second round, and Ransconsi had struggled frantically to free it; but when he had removed the source of the trouble — grit from the desert in the breech — it came to life with devastating effect.

The Arabs couldn't stand that swift-firing little weapon, deadly at close quarters. Ransconsi came raging in among the camels, shrieking hell and furies upon the wretches who dared to attack the glorious Legion. His revolver thundered, and the attack faded away.

The survivors loped off on their camels, or crawled away into the desert to nurse their wounds. The little party stood, recovering from the fierceness of that ordeal, looking at each other through the sweat that filled their eyes with acid pain.

Then Arabs, dismounted and lying up in the sand, began to fire vengeful shots in among the group, and that brought their weary limbs into action again.

Ransconsi, superb in this moment of physical danger, shouted to his men to begin their march again. He put four men to the rear to shoot down any Arabs who rose from cover as they marched out of range.

Five men had been lost in that melée. They were left in the desert, though their rifles were carefully collected and taken with the surviving legionnaires. That was one of the first things a legionnaire was taught — 'Never leave a rifle where an enemy can find it.'

The wounded were slung between their more fortunate comrades. For never did the Legion leave its injured if it was possible to take them with them. Injured legionnaires received no mercy at the hands of their enemies, they all knew.

Nicky insisted on walking alone, now. The way was uphill, and she didn't want to tax her friends' strength if she could avoid it. Perhaps that rest during the fighting with the camel men had helped her. Or perhaps gallantly she drew upon those final reserves of strength, which are within us all and can be mastered in the most critical of moments.

Somehow she staggered on, keeping pace with the toiling band of legionnaires. Sometimes men stumbled and plunged headfirst into the hot sand. Sometimes they were so weary that they lay where they were, as if the danger that lying there brought to them was less than the torrent of trying once more to resume that agonising march.

Then rough-handed but compassionate comrades swore at them and dragged them into the march again.

They were climbing, half a mile from the ridge top now. Nicky suddenly gripped Tex's arm and pointed silently west of them.

That mighty Arab horde had thundered down off the long, bare ridge and was racing into the basin towards them. They were only a mile or so away.

And the camel men, like vultures, were closing in on them again. Five only left now on their racing camels, but they had speed and were near, and now they were racing in for a further suicidal attack.

Ransconsi shouted a command. The wounded were dropped; rifles came up to shoulders that were almost without the strength to hold them. A crash of fire sent the camel men spinning away, clinging to their saddles when they were injured, and toppling off when their strength gave out.

A scream of fury rose from that thundering mass of Arabs, pounding down the basin towards them. The legionnaires, stumbling forward once again, saw the many-coloured robes of the desert warriors streaming in the breeze; saw white and black and brown horseflesh in the van of an army that merged into the up-thrown dust from kicking hooves in the van of the onslaught.

Nicky sobbed, suddenly: 'We'll never make it, Tex!'

Tex grabbed her under the arm and kept her going. The howling, frenzied mass of mounted Arabs came wheeling in to the attack. It was like using a mighty pile-driver to crack a nut, thought Tex cynically. This army, several thousand strong, would annihilate them within seconds, in spite of their modern Lebel rifles and better military training.

Ransconsi was a raging fury, leading them. They had come so far, and now it seemed they were to suffer defeat almost in the shadow of safety. That column of legionnaires could only be a half-mile or so beyond the ridge top, must have heard the sounds of that running battle this last twenty minutes or so . . . unless all during this time they had resumed their head-long flight northwards again.

Suddenly Ransconsi saw that the end was near. That horde of yelling Arabs was less than two hundred yards from them. They saw the flash of swords in the sunlight, saw the crazy exultation on those long, narrow Arab faces, and knew they were within seconds of death.

Ransconsi, typically, gave the order to fight to the end.

He shouted out a string of orders. The

wounded went down with a crash again. Those able to handle rifles knelt beside their prostrate comrades and began to fire viciously at these Arabs who intended to butcher them.

Tex was with them, rifle to his shoulder. He saw a blurred mass, and knew he couldn't miss — and knew it would make no difference if he did hit with every bullet.

This was the end . . .

The whole front of the attacking Arabs somersaulted and went down. Horses piled on top of horses; men went under, engulfed by the maelstrom of struggling flesh and blood. And more men and more horses went down behind them.

The exultant screams of those charging Arabs took on a different note. Fear entered into it, fear and even panic.

For seconds that astonished band of legionnaires watched a mad struggle to pull charging horses away from that piled up tangle of dead and dying men and horseflesh. The dust rose higher and grew thicker, so that events were seen through a deepening grey-yellow fog.

They saw, though, that mighty army waver, then pull aside, and then go circling off in a line that seemed endless behind its screen of desert dust. And no longer was it a triumphant army, but one uncertain and made cautious by the injuries it had received.

Ransconsi had to come storming among his men to shake them from the stupefaction that seemed to have gripped them. They couldn't understand it. Half a minute before, their end had seemed certain. Now it was the Arab army that was retreating and leaving them alone on the battlefield. Dazed, they looked at their Lebels and wondered if their guns had taken on a magical deadliness to protect them.

Then the sergeant-major shattered their vague speculation with his usual brutal directness.

He stamped in, swearing and shouting. He was pointing. They followed the direction of his finger with their weary, incredulous eyes.

That ridge behind them was a bristling line of heads and rifles. Heads topped by white kepis, neck curtains fluttering in the breeze that stirred up on that height.

Ransconsi was almost screaming, '*Voila*, we are saved! We have won through, my children! They used us as bait to bring the Arabs within range of their guns. Now let us go with all haste into the safety of their ranks!'

An officer was standing up on the ridge, shouting down to them. The legionnaires threw off their trance-like astonishment, picked up their comrades and began to climb the hill.

When they were within a hundred yards of the top, rifle bullets began to spatter after them, from the defeated, vengeful Arabs in the valley below. They did no damage and served only to accelerate the pace of those weary, struggling legionnaires.

When Ransconsi and his men were within a hundred yards of their comrades on top of the ridge, someone began to cheer the little band of struggling men. The cheer swept all along the line. And then excited legionnaires came plunging down to meet them, in spite of the ferocious bellowings of their officers; they took hold of the wounded and helped them up the last yards into safety.

Ransconsi loved it. He disdained all assistance and went marching up as if he had all the strength in the world. A sergeant-major of the Legion was not going to parade weakness in front of the canaille who populated it. He came in with jaw sticking belligerently forward, eyes flashing, and arms swinging. He saw an officer, and gave him a magnificent salute.

And then, to the delight of his men who saw a tyrant in the Italian as well as an iron man, poor Ransconsi collapsed.

The rest of the party collapsed, too. They were dragged behind the breastworks that had been thrown up along the summit of this ridge, then lay where they were placed tenderly on the soft sand.

Men came running up with precious water to revive them, and blankets were stretched across sticks so as to provide shade for them. They lay there, with admiring legionnaires to look down on them and congratulate them on their good fortune in being alive. Among them were the darker-faced Colonial troops, conscripted Arab Tirailleurs and Senegalese, in boots that were too big for them, with blue puttees trailing round their ankles because they would not hold up on those thin, native legs.

Then officers shouted furious orders, and leather-lunged N.C.O.s relayed them, only on an even more savage note. At that the emotional legionnaires, who had been excited beyond the point of endurance by this race for life, returned to their defensive positions on the edge of the ridge.

They lay together, Nicky with these men who were her comrades now because they had shared a common peril together; the thick blanket cast a welcome shade above them, and they lay with eyes closed, indifferent to the events around them.

The officers came to look upon them, aroused by the whisper that there was a lovely young girl with this party of legionnaires. But though they stood and made their frank comments about her, neither Nicky nor her companions opened their eyes — hardly heard them, anyway, and weren't concerned by what was said if they did hear them.

There was no fighting after that, not until after sunset, anyway. The fiery sun declined steadily, losing its heat gradually. All along that flat-topped ridge the French troops strengthened their defences while light lasted and prepared for the siege that was inevitable.

Late that afternoon Tex awoke from a sleep, astonishingly refreshed. He heard the hum of conversation around him, and began to piece together the situation.

This was a defeated French force that had been driven from possession of an oasis forty miles to the west of them. They had seen the inevitable end to their attempt to hold on to the oasis, and had abandoned the place early one night, soon after darkness.

They had struck eastwards, in an effort to reach the safety of the line of French defences near to the Mediterranean coast, and luck had been with them. A sandstorm had sprung up during the first hours of their march, obliterating their tracks and so hampering the Arabs when they came to look for their enemies.

But inevitably fast-riding Arab scouts had at length picked up their trail and, as they saw, brought the main Arab force on after them. The French commander, a Foreign Legion colonel, had seen the hopelessness of attempting to outdistance the Arabs — cavalry was still faster than marching men even on this sandy desert — and deliberately he had chosen to make a stand on this ridged plateau. The steep approach from all sides would discount some of the manoeuvrability of the Arab horsemen, and his much smaller force was ordered to dig trenches all along the face of the ridge.

And the French colonel had permitted the struggling little band of legionnaires under Ransconsi to lure the over-eager enemy within reach of his column's bitter, vengeful guns. That fusillade which had saved the lives of Ransconsi and his men had taken heavy toll of the Arab Nationalists. Now they were encamped back at a distance, probably resting before resuming the attack on their hated enemies.

Tex rose, his bones full of weariness

still. Yet he knew that with the cool of night his strength would return swiftly to him. The Legion was hard upon its men, but it gave them a stamina that enabled them very swiftly to throw off fatigue.

Field kitchens had been set up, and he tramped across and asked for food, for he had eaten nothing all that day. They were kind to him, and treated him as a hero — a condition that wouldn't last, he knew — and gave him muddy soup made from horse flesh, and a hunk of iron-hard brown bread. It tasted good. That horse had been one that had died in the skirmish with the Arabs, and was therefore fresh meat. Then they gave him a cup of sour wine, and it revived him and made him feel suddenly fit and well again.

He took soup and wine back to his companions. Rube was lying with one eye open, beginning to take an interest in life. Joe Ellighan was on his back still, making hideous noises through his wide-open mouth.

Tex gently wakened Nicky and gave her soup and bread. She went back to sleep again immediately. A runner came up, then, to order Tex to report to the officers. He was surprised that he should be singled out so, but he told Rube to watch over Nicky and see that none of these rough legionnaires got offensive with her, and then he went off with the runner.

He tramped along that ridge. He saw that the column consisted of about two hundred men, and that all were lying quietly on the edges of the long, narrow plateau. A trench had been dug that connected round the edge of the flattened ridge, and seeing the men crouching there, watching down the loose, sandy slopes, he thought that the Arabs would find this defence position a tough nut to crack.

Then he looked down into the valley, where the Arab Nationalist army was encamped, and he gasped. Spread out like a town was the huge force of Arabs — thousands of them. Tex saw a number of tents being put up, as if a slower baggage train had arrived after the main force. And everywhere were horses, tied or hobbled so as to keep them near to their owners, who sat in colourful groups for miles across the flattened bottom of the basin.

He looked north and east of them. Strong parties of Arabs sat their horses on distant ridges. This time the Arabs weren't going to let their prey sneak away from them when night fell. The two-hundred-strong French force was surrounded by thousands of militant Arabs.

Tex thought: 'If they've got sense, they'll just sit there an' wait until our water runs out. Then they've got us without losing a man.'

But he knew that army leaders didn't usually run to sense. Men like Nuhas Pasha, the Arab leader, preferred the spectacular to the unpretentious, however sensible the latter. He would want deeds that stirred the blood and gave opportunity in the bazaars for men to boast afterwards — those fortunate men who survived.

'He'll send his men charging in regardless of the cost,' thought Tex. 'He'll reckon on swamping this force by sheer weight of numbers.'

But he could see the strength of this defensive position, and he thought that Nuhas Pasha, the Arab Nationalist war leader, was going to get a shock when the attack was launched.

The French officers had got all this worked out, too. That was why they had sent for Tex and several other legionnaires. They were in conference under a fly sheet that gave protection from the last rays of the reluctantly setting sun while inviting a cooling current of air under its edges.

Tex saw the colonel, an old, greymoustached man, with eyes that had faded almost colourless through a life on the desert. He was stiff-legged in his breeches and even now, polished leggings; an old man who had fought so long in the desert that even his dulled and obstinate brain held some notions of strategy.

There were other, brighter young officers around him to prompt him in the situation that faced them. Mostly they were beautifully dressed young men who rarely faced the rigours of life beyond

Sidi-bel-Illah and other garrison towns on the coast. This war springing up suddenly in the desert was not to their liking, and they had complained loudly about the hardships of the campaign, which had gone so much against them.

Even so, fops though many were, they had intelligence and some military training, and they were applying themselves to the problem of ensuring their own survival.

They knew the inevitability of Arab attack, because that was the unvarying Arab tactic. But they were looking beyond; for unless they looked into the future and measured their strategy accordingly, there could be but one end to this siege upon the plateau in the desert.

Tex found Ransconsi there, as tough-looking and ferocious-eyed as ever. Four other legionnaires came up simultaneously with him. They were from another regiment, and he didn't know them.

The colonel looked at them without expression in his faded grey eyes, and spoke with the slow deliberation of an old man. They had been summoned, he said, because they could speak and understand Arabic.

Tex sighed inwardly. This had happened before. If information was needed from Arabs, le Legionnaire Texas, who was a formidable linguist, was invariably selected to go out in Arab dress and keep his big ears open.

'Soon,' continued that old colonel, who should have been pensioned off years before, but had refused retirement because for him there was no life outside an army, 'these mutinous dogs of Arabs will mount an attack. They will be repelled, because they will be hot-headed and foolish. After that they will make other, cleverer plans to dislodge us, and we must know what those plans are so that we can counter them.

'Therefore, children of France, you will go out, dressed as Arabs, when there is opportunity for you to do so with safety. Perhaps with the darkness, when the defeated Arabs go back to attend to their wounds and bury their dead. But that is for you to decide. Sufficient is it that we must have information of the enemy's intentions, for I see no way of escape from our situation except by a miracle founded upon good intelligence.'

With that he dismissed them. He wanted to lie down now on the bed that his ordinance had erected for him, and he felt that he had spoken enough.

Tex began to tramp back towards his companions. His thoughts were grim. This desert was hell enough without men making survival even more difficult. He racked his brains to try to think of some way out of this desperate situation, for himself and friends — especially for this girl, Nicky, who had come to mean so much in his life — if not for these comrades of the Legion, yet there was apparently no way out for them.

Their future seemed to be dictated by this mighty throng of blood-crazed Arabs — yet Tex didn't find it in his heart to condemn them for what they were doing now.

He knew Arab life all too well. Knew it so well that he knew he too would have been out there with those Arabs if he had been born in this relentless, inhospitable

Sahara. War was a godsend to them — any excuse to break with the dreary routine of scratching a living where Nature was all against men surviving.

When the call came to arms, men didn't consider the motives behind the call or the consequences to themselves of entering upon a war. Instead they were ready to follow anyone who could make an inflammatory speech.

Not that there wasn't excuse enough for inflammatory speeches, Tex thought, approaching their blanket shelter. Life was made hard by the desert conditions of their country, but a rapacious, indolent and inefficient system oppressed them in a thousand different ways and added to the burdens that Nature imposed upon them.

He heard a sound. Turned. Two lieutenants were catching up on him. They were young and bold, made confident by their conquests in the salons along the coast towns. When they saw the big American pause, they exchanged quick glances and then came directly up towards him.

He saluted. One eyed him haughtily, with contempt; for that was the approved officer-treatment for legionnaires in the Legion.

'It is said that an American girl came in with your party, legionnaire.'

'That is true, *mon officier*,' murmured Tex, his eyes watching the two men intently.

'Lead us to this girl,' the officer said haughtily, and at that Tex said: 'Very well, *mon officier*,' and turned and went on to where his friends awaited him.

He was not to be deceived. These officers knew the girl was there, because they had been among the bold-eyed officers who had gathered round them in their exhaustion upon their arrival. They were up to some trick, he knew, and he didn't trust these killers of garrison-town butterflies.

Rube and other men who were awake scrambled to their feet when the officers trudged up through the soft sand. That wakened Nicky, who sat up in their midst in the shadow cast by that blanket.

She looked tired still, and her blouse

and slacks showed the marks of long travel; yet she looked young and fresh-looking and very desirable in the presence of those rough, scrub-chinned legionnaires.

Tex saw the officers' eyes glint with pleasure at sight of her. His heart sank. Here was trouble, and he had been ordered out of the camp and couldn't stand by the girl when she needed him.

The other officer spoke, in a voice that was painfully high-pitched and immature. But he wanted to show off before this attractive foreign girl. Was it not said that all American girls had riches as well as charm?

'Mad'moiselle, it is not fit that you should lie on the sand amid all these rough soldiers,' he said eagerly. 'See, we have a tent, and we place it at your disposal.' His hand indicated the few tents at the far end of the narrow plateau.

Nicky looked at Tex, her blue eyes calculating. She wasn't going to put herself in the power of amorous young officers, if she could help it.

Tex spoke with an abruptness that spoke eloquently of his opinion of their intentions. 'Mad'moiselle has come to no harm from these rough soldiers, *mon officier*. Perhaps it is as well that they continue to look after her.'

'Silence,' thundered the young whipper-snapper. 'It is for us, in our superior wisdom, to decide such matters. Go, miserable wretch, and prepare yourself for your expedition, as the colonel ordered.'

Those words brought a leaping fear into Nicky's blue eyes, but she withheld her questions on that subject for a moment and merely said: 'It is for me to decide, surely, *m'sieur*. And I have no wish for a tent; rather I intend to stay with these gallant legionnaires who have looked so well after me until now.'

The officers were visibly shaken by those words. They had never expected that their gallantry might be spurned in such a decisive way. They even felt indignation rising under their well-tailored uniforms. They, officers of the Legion, were being turned down in favour of the society of crude ill-favoured infantrymen who had nothing to offer a girl. Now, they . . .

They protested. Perhaps mad'moiselle

did not understand what they were offering? Mad'moiselle surely did not know what she was saying. They had a bed for her, a tent; an ordinance would look after her and bring her food that a lady could enjoy and not this swill that was good only for pigs of legionnaires.

Tex's eyes glinted enjoyment as he heard a New York drawl say, laconically: 'Sure, and what would you boys want out of it?'

They'd want to make love to her, of course; would expect it from her as of right if she accepted their hospitality. No doubt they had pictured the delicious situation of themselves the envy of their brother officers, the champions of a delightful and grateful American girl.

They'd even forgotten that threatening Arab army in that thought; or perhaps their ego wouldn't let them believe that here was to be an end to their young lives. In between the fighting would be admiring blue eyes, giving credit for their gallantry, they had mentally decided. Only now they were receiving an unexpected setback to their plans.

This girl was saying 'No' to their offer in her own language as well as theirs.

The officers caught the grins on the faces of the stubble-chinned soldiery around them. The legionnaires were enjoying this discomfiture; it was not often they had the pleasure of seeing their superior officers put in their places.

They persisted, not really believing they were being rejected. And they suffered yet a further humbling to their pride. But there came a point when the officers had to recognise defeat, and red-faced with shame they turned and stalked away.

Tex sighed and turned towards the girl. 'Honey, you sure put those boys in their places. They had a mean look in their eyes.'

'It's meaner now,' Nicky laughed.

Rube looked at his comrade, Tex, and said, warningly: 'I don't trust officers — not young ones — where a girl's concerned. Better watch out for yourself, Tex.'

'Meanin'?'

Rube shrugged. 'Maybe they might get you away from Nicky so's to leave her alone an' unprotected. Get you put under arrest, for instance, or stick you under guard for bein' insolent or insubordinate or any old thing.'

Tex said: 'Yeah, yeah. But where I'm goin', those guys can't do much for me.'

He told his comrades and Nicky his orders. The girl was horrified. 'You've . . . to go in among those Arabs? Oh, Tex, if they recognise you . . . '

Tex shrugged. He had to see they didn't recognise him. He looked at Rube and the pug-faced Joe Ellighan. 'Brothers, when I go out, you keep watch on Nicky for me? Okay?'

'To the end,' said Rube grimly, and it made Tex feel easier in his mind to hear that said.

Then they all sat down to await the expected Arab attack. It came in the last half-hour of daylight, at a time when the sun, almost eclipsed in the west, cast great patches of shadow across the undulating ground. Suddenly, as if from nowhere, a horde of Arab cavalry came spurring out from a depression to the northeast of them. There must have been four hundred in that assault alone, and immediately it began the rest of the Arab thousands came storming in to the attack from all sides.

The Arabs had hoped to crash in among the defenders before they realised that an attack had started; their plan had been to occupy the French troops at close quarters while the rest of the Arab Nationalist force poured in for the final slaughter.

But an alert defence, anticipating this move, began a vicious fire upon the attackers almost from the moment they appeared from out of the shadows. Then, too, that slope to the defended plateau proved arduous beyond anticipation, and it slowed the attack and left the fanatically yelling Arab cavalry at the mercy of the well-armed, better disciplined troops on the ridge.

Even so, because of their numbers that attack almost overwhelmed the besieged little force. In the gathering darkness the burnoused Arab force seemed like an irresistible flood. They saw the charging mass apparently unaffected by the bullets they pumped in among the attackers;

their ears rang to the frenzy of shouted war cries from the Arab warriors and the frightened screams of horses that all too often were felled by bullets intended for the riders.

Then, around most of the ridge, the attack was beaten off. Almost when it seemed those ferocious cavalrymen would ride the last few yards up to the summit and break in upon them, the attack wavered in face of that deadly fire from the blue-tunicked men in the trenches.

The Arabs saw only spitting guns that crashed death among them; the defence seemed inhuman, killing silently, which is not the Arab way. That cold, remorseless slaughter put them in a panic. A few couldn't face those death-dealing Lebels, and they pulled their horses away and tried to escape across the face of the slope.

That action had the effect that it always has upon charging cavalry. Those behind, not understanding the reason for the change of course, automatically followed . . . and the attack petered out. The Arab cavalry rode madly out of range, and then milled around in a confused mass half a mile away in the bottom of the valley.

The Arabs came back to collect their dead and dying, and there were hundreds. It had been a terrible loss to the rebellious Nationalists.

In the northern sector the Arab attack did ride right in among the defenders. There a resolute band of cavalry kept on up the slope when it seemed that nothing could live under that withering fire from the legionnaires. About fifty hacked their way through the line of defenders, then began to ride like furies along the ridge, calling to their people outside to resume the attack.

For a few seconds the defenders didn't understand what had happened — it looked as if they were being overwhelmed, and they came jumping out of their trenches, rifles swinging in a desperate hand-to-hand effort to beat off the attack.

For a few minutes the battle raged, then one by one those brave but impetuous horsemen were dragged from their saddles and killed, or were shot off their mounts.

All at once there was silence, save for

the groans of the wounded and dying. Night was still a few minutes away, and they could see, if indistinctly.

The plateau was a shambles. The N.C.O.s at once came running up, shouting to the men to throw the Arab corpses down the hillside, and get the defences ready for further attack.

But there was no other attack upon the position that night. It had been a mad, reckless plan, in any event, and hundreds of Arabs had died because their leader had wanted the glory of being a victorious general in battle.

There was exultation among the defenders on the ridge, for most had survived, because of their protective trenches, unscratched. Then gradually the thrill of victory ebbed as they took stock of their position.

Defeat in the end seemed certain for them. The Arabs didn't need to fire another gun to overwhelm them. All they need do was to sit around the hill and wait until the defenders' water ran out and the hot Sahara sun sent the French troops crazy with thirst. Within an hour of victory, pessimism was rife among the defenders; for they knew that those would be the tactics of the badly-mauled Arab army from now on.

Tex wasn't among them. Burnoused like an Arab he had slipped out with the retreating throng when the first attack failed. All night they kept watch for him, but he never showed up.

Then, three hours before dawn a blue-eyed man in Arab costume was brought in by the sentries. He spoke with the colonel. In a few minutes there was silent activity all along the ridge. Then all watched into the valley, and when they saw the sign they marched swiftly away.

When Tex did return, that column had gone, had disappeared like water in the shifting sands of the desert. And Nicky and his friends had gone, too.

11

Roast Him Alive!

No one took any notice of Tex as he trekked across the valley towards the main encampment of the Arab army. All around him were men on horseback, searching for comrades among the fallen; unhorsed Arabs returned silently on foot, some with dragging steps that spoke of wounds and injuries. Tex wasn't at all conspicuous and was able to walk openly and upright through the darkness towards the distant fires.

When he reached the town of tents, it seemed that the place had gone mad. There was a roaring sound that grew steadily louder as he approached. It was the sound of men in anger, all talking and getting more heated in their talk with the passing moments.

It was the sound of a defeated army, anxious to pass on some of its sufferings and feelings of ignominy to others.

Tex came out where dozens of little fires and hundreds of blazing torches lit up the tented area of the encampment. The red light fell on swarthy faces and reflected in a curiously baleful manner from the flashing, angry eyes of squatting nomads.

Tex pulled his Arab cloak closer around him; his chin was buried in the mouth cloth of his hooded burnouse, so that only his eyes were revealed to betray him. These he kept as narrowed as possible, so that a brown-eyed people wouldn't see that this tall Arab's eyes were grey.

He walked down between the fires, listening to the talk of the groups around them. Now men were wiser after the event. These Arabs were saying that only a madman and a fool would have ordered such a reckless charge upon their deadly enemies. If they had but sat in their tents and waited, wouldn't the good Allah have delivered up their enemies to them without so much as one lost life? they demanded indignantly.

They forgot to say that they had

welcomed the order to go out and do battle; for sitting in their tents is no Arab way of conducting a war. Now humbled by that infinitely smaller force, conscious of the terrible thrashing they had received, they sought only to blame their leaders for what they had urged upon them themselves.

Tex moved on. The talk was the same at every fire.

Until he came upon a Tormented Man.

He came to one group that was silent listening to a quiet voice that spoke convincingly though without passion. Tex moved closer, then became rigid, hearing what was being said. Here were words rarely spoken in the Arab world; things were being said that weren't often understood among a primitive, warring people.

'This war can end only in disaster. We are but puny striplings compared with the mighty French giant. They have men in their millions if need be and they can bring tanks and great guns — they have the dreaded machine guns and rifles that outrange our own poor weapons.

'What is courage against spinning lead and bayonets? What good will it do us if we do wipe out this tiny force of infidels? I say, end this war, for victory tomorrow will bring sorrow to our villages. The French will not forget . . . '

The moon was rising, to add light to that of the flaming torches and the glowing fires of dried camel dung. The speaker in the circle around that fire turned slightly, and Tex saw his face. It seemed familiar A few seconds later he remembered where he had seen it before.

This was one of the Brotherhood of Tormented Men. He was here among the Arab troops, talking against this war with the French.

Tex walked away. Now he sought only those circles where men listened quietly, and at every one he found one of the Brethren holding forth.

They talked against the war as being suicide, and then they began to talk against the war leaders.

'We are fools to listen to their voices.' It was the old, old man who had so much compassion in his tortured frame that he could bring water to an enemy as hated as Captain Sturmer, of the French Foreign Legion. Tex heard his direct speech, and thought: 'This man has courage beyond my own.' For though these Arabs were sore from defeat, yet they must have a residing loyalty to their leaders, and to speak so boldly against them seemed to invite disaster.

'Do our war leaders ever suffer the way we who follow must suffer?' There were murmurs around the fire. 'If they are defeated they retire with their fortunes to foreign lands, but we cannot follow them there — we must stay and face the wrath of the enemies they have made. We must pay the taxes to cover the cost of the war, and always we must look upon the faces of our arrogant conquerors.

'It is easy for these rich and powerful sheiks and pashas to call us to arms. They have everything to gain and apparently nothing to lose by attempts to overthrow the hated French. But it is we who have to do the fighting, we who get hurt and die.' Suddenly, without warning, that old man rapped a question — 'When did you hear of a war leader getting wounded — or being killed in wartime, except by accident?'

Again murmurs growled approval of what he said. A harsh, embittered voice called from behind the circle; 'Their lives are too valuable to be risked in battle. That is what they tell us.' A pause, then in anguish: 'But my son was encouraged to go forth with his sword.'

Tex looked over the heads of the crowd. He saw the speaker, an elderly Arab who sat by a still white huddle that was once a man. An old man in misery, grieving over his loss, and seeing the truth through the pain of sorrow.

But not all men there were against war. Some spoke up fiercely and called that old Tormented Man a traitor and a renegade and a man in the pay of France. The old man listened but only shook his head, and they knew that he wasn't.

A few rose angrily and stamped away, because they had been taught to follow without question, and the old man's words made a demand upon their powers to reason and they didn't want to start thinking at their age.

Yet other men twisted the words of the Tormented Men who spoke against war — twisted them to their way of liking. Tex, standing silently on the fringe of the crowds, his hand under his burnouse gripping the revolver that was his sole weapon — a revolver reluctantly donated by Ransconsi up there on the ridge upon the imperative demands of their colonel — Tex began to understand this new undercurrent of talk that began to spread among the Arabs.

It was all true, these Arabs began to murmur. That suicidal assault upon the ridge had been the folly of a man unfit to lead men. Nuhas Pasha had grown senile in luxurious exile in Egypt; no longer was he the warrior chief that he had once been.

Then the whispers began to mention another name, and that brought further understanding to Tex — understanding and hope. Men of the desert needed nomad leaders, these Arabs began to say with increasing loudness. Such a man was Sheik Mahmoud ibn Kalim ibn Hussein ibn Achmet el Dusa, they declared. Was he not a desert fox, wise in the ways of warfare because he had never stopped fighting the French even during the days of 'peace'? Had he not inspired this rebellion and led it with success until the arrival of Nuhas Pasha from Egypt? Nuhas had taken over leadership because of his old reputation, yet see the folly of the man — he could have wiped out this force without striking a blow, yet he had incurred such losses that the villages within a thousand miles would resound to the wailing of women lamenting their dead.

Tex heard the talk and saw the way it went and knew it for the everlasting intrigue that goes where power is to be held. These whisperers were followers of the deposed Sheik Mahmoud, that thin-faced, hungry-eyed man who coveted power above all other things in life. Their fortunes were bound with his, and, no doubt acting under orders from their powerful chief, they were talking against their arrogant leader, Nuhas Pasha, in an attempt to overthrow him.

His pulse quickening, because this opened up possibilities for him, Tex listened to the growing whispers, and noted how they were taken up and passed on from fire to fire. Sheik Mahmoud's men were out in force, seeking desperately to take advantage of this moment and bring other men to their side.

Then he began to walk towards the bigger tents, where the noble Arabs would be reclining, seeking solace perhaps in the Western habit of alcohol that was forbidden by their religion. As he pushed his way through the stirring, excited throng that had suddenly become conscious of the imminence of startling events, he realised that the voice of the Tormented Men, speaking against war and against all war leaders, was eclipsed now by louder mouths who called openly for a change in leadership — and put the name of the crafty, merciless Sheik Mahmoud upon their lips.

Only one voice talked against them, and talked as loudly. Tex felt a thrill course through his body as he heard that voice coming to him from the distance.

It was Suleiman's — Suleiman the Hideous, the enigma, the man who fascinated him because out of his torment had come this passionate determination to help the afflicted against their oppressors.

Suleiman was standing out there, risking his life because he spoke the truth as he knew it. Tex didn't know it, but he was talking desperately against this whisper campaign to put Sheik Mahmoud where Nuhas Pasha stood — and keep the war on against the French.

'Mahmoud or Nuhas,' Suleiman's voice rang out clearly. 'Either will bring you to disaster. You fools, going to your deaths on the legionnaires' bayonets will not help your cause. We of the Arab world will be weakened by our losses, and weakening us strengthens our enemies.

'Do not listen to our leaders who talk of war, for they are bigger enemies to the *fellahin* than the French oppressors. No, I say, turn ears that are deaf to this talk of further war. Remember the suffering it has brought already, and mount your horses and ride back to your fields, to your wives and children, to your mothers and old fathers. The shadow of Allah is upon you all tonight, and in his name I cry peace — peace for the people who have so little of it. Peace even if it is under the heel of a tyrant oppressor.'

Tex was close by the biggest, most elaborate of the tents now. Of course the leaders had their comfort, even in wartime; here, in the middle of the Sahara, their tents would be brought to them, and the cushions and hangings that gave them a comfort known to few of their followers at any time.

The curtains were back, showing the colourful interior, the drapes and the carpets all revealed in the light of silver oil lamps. Men were squatting within, important men by their richer costume. These would be the lieutenants of Nuhas Pasha, the Arab Nationalist leader, Tex was thinking, and then he caught sight of the man himself.

Tex had met Nuhas once before. The Arab was a fine-looking man just entering on to middle age. A handsome, intelligent Arab, bold and resourceful, Nuhas Pasha was yet a man who looked upon opportunity as his own. He could not forget his breed and birth, and in consequence he had come to regard all other men as inferior to him. These men who obeyed his call and rode into battle were yet cattle in his opinion, though he was clever enough not to show this cynicism before his followers. Now, when he heard the cries against his leadership, he became arrogant and intolerant against those who questioned his will.

Tex became aware of the quick coming and going into the council tent of well-armed Arab tribesmen. He began to see that these were the picked bodyguard of Nuhas Pasha, and they would be coming in to make their reports upon an explosive situation developing outside. That council was discussing the threat to their rule — no doubt discussing it and planning to circumvent the danger.

In the far distance, where a great throng was gathering to hear the bold haranguer, where torches flamed closely together, Tex heard the clear, ringing tones of Suleiman the Hideous, Suleiman calling upon men to cling to their senses and not listen to any further talk of war. He was still talking against a change of leadership. If a new leader meant a continuation of this war that could only end in disaster for the desert warriors, then they should not listen to this whispering campaign.

That was Suleiman's theme. There were men to shout against it now, and they were the men of Sheik Mahmoud's faction who were as much opposed to talk of peace as they were to a continuance of Nuhas Pasha's reign as chief.

Suleiman talked back at them, but while he had many who secretly knew in their hearts that his was the more acceptable policy, they were loath to stand up and say so. For it is traditional that an Arab male should be a fighting man, and none wanted to go back to their womenfolk bearing the label of one who ran away from an enemy.

Tex caught a heightening in the tension, felt that Suleiman's bold words were precipitating a situation. Now men were running from Nuhas Pasha's tent and finding comrades and bringing them closer in to where the chiefs planned a bold stroke to outwit their enemies. Tex had to go back, deeper among the tents, so as to avoid getting involved with the concentrating bodyguard.

Then he looked across to the darker, desert tents of the nomad chief, Sheik Mahmoud el Dusa. Silent groups of men were clustered about them, their horses picketed close to hand. Tex knew they were watching and awaiting developments, ready to reveal their hand if it seemed that Fortune was riding Sheik Mahmoud's way.

Then he found that others were watching and listening. Instinct suddenly alerted him to the presence of a hovering Arab who clung to the shadows to the rear of Nuhas Pasha's big tent. Tex watched him for a while, and then became certain that this was no Arab, for when the man moved, as he had to at times, he strode out quickly under his long burnoused cloak . . . and an Arab, used to the restrictions of his dress, moves always in small strides and never attempts to stride out, as does a man used to army pantaloons or trousers.

So, because he was seeing into the future now, was planning to shape it to some extent, Tex went up and spoke to the man. The man was startled. Tex gripped him to keep him quiet.

'Quiet,' he whispered. 'I too am of the Legion, *mon petit*.'

He felt the relaxation of muscles as the spy in Arab clothing realised that here was no danger. Tex began to whisper in his ear. 'Soon,' he was saying, 'all Arab forces will be here where their leaders are. Men will not stay out in the desert when fighting flares up in the main camp.'

'You think they will fight?' The man's voice barely reached his ears.

'They will fight,' said Tex with certainty. 'That will bring in the Arabs who now surround the Legion. Go, thou, and tell the colonel to march out and escape with his men when he sees disaster strike the Arab camp.'

The man nodded, then walked quietly away into the darkness. The big, lean American watched him go, then his eyes looked for allies among his enemies.

He had to work fast. By the sound of things, tempers were working up among the crowd. Soon they would break, and then the rival factions would begin the struggle for power.

But Tex didn't want a gradual development of this struggle. He planned the spectacular, something that would bring in every Arab for miles around. For he knew that the one thing that would unite these contending forces immediately would be news that the hated Frank was escaping.

There must be no Arab watcher left out there alongside the moonlit ridge to bring in warning.

He began to push through the jostling throng of excited, arguing Arabs. Once someone caught him by the arm and tried to get his opinion on a point, but Tex roughly threw away the grip and walked on like a man who has an important purpose in mind.

He had. He was looking for the Brethren of Tormented Men — those men who lived now only for the end of those autocrats and tyrants who lived by the misery of Arab-land's oppressed millions.

Suleiman was still talking back to the crowd, still talking boldly against this war and against all war leaders. Tex caught a glimpse of a group of well-attired Arabs pushing their way through the throng towards Suleiman the Bold, and he knew what that meant. They looked like the personal bodyguard of Nuhas Pasha.

It made him feel panicky, made him more urgent in his search — and less cautious. Almost frantically now he pushed through the crowd, searching for a man with a bad memory in his eyes . . .

He found that old, old man, squatting out of tiredness by a fire now deserted save for himself and an old man who was saying what a fine son he had lost that night, and how he had lost five sons in three wars and now there was none left.

Tex came down beside that old, old man, that Tormented Man who could yet feel compassion for another's suffering. He saw the wrinkled old face turn towards his . . . and realised that he had been recognised.

Before he could speak, there was a savage roar from the big crowd where Suleiman had been speaking. Tex came to his feet, dragging that old man with him. He kept a grip on that tattered old *galabier*, because now more than ever it was imperative that he shouldn't lose this link with the Brotherhood, here amid the enemy.

The crowd surged and swayed in the meaningless way that mobs do when they are impelled by throat-gripping excitement and all want to see yet cannot, not at the same time.

Tex pushed out his free hand as sandalled feet came back to tread on his own, and white-robed desert warriors were thrown against him by the swaying crowd. Then he found himself caught in the tide of that crowd's movement. They were swirling towards the big tent that was a monument to the splendour of Nuhas Pasha.

Big Tex struggled, tried to break out from the throng, but found himself unable to do so at that moment. The old man went meekly with him, as if it wasn't in his aged bones to protest at any sort of manhandling.

Gradually Tex began to see what was happening. Nuhas Pasha's bodyguard had seized this bold interloper who dared to speak against sheiks and pashas and were dragging him towards the tent of their chief. The crowd was following, not sure where their sympathies lay, but impelled by curiosity to witness the treatment meted out to this big, hideous-visaged beggar from the city gutters.

Tex caught occasional glimpses of the tall Arab who had once plotted his death, and in spite of everything he felt an attraction towards the man — he felt the man's dignity even now when he was a prisoner and was being hustled so unceremoniously along; somehow even now, across the heads of that excited, milling crowd under the moon and the flaming torches, he felt the strength of the man's personality, his fearlessness, his certainty that what he had done was right, whatever fate came to him in consequence.

The crowd came to a halt before that

long, low tent that was the Arab chief's battle headquarters. The front had been uncurtained, so that the rude Arab tribesmen could see the splendours of the carpet on the floor, the rich colours of the drapes on the back wall, and the gleaming silver and ornaments that had been brought for their chief's pleasure here in the desert.

Nuhas Pasha was there, sitting alone on a pile of richly embroidered cushions — a fine-looking man, calm and at ease before the throng. His advisers and chiefs of staff stood respectfully back, as players do to the leading actor in a stage drama. It was a good thing not to try to share the limelight with a powerful chief like Nuhas Pasha.

Fanning out on either side of the entrance to the tent, keeping the sand clear for fifty yards before their chief, was the picked guard of Nuhas Pasha — men who had ridden with him from his exile in Egypt, big, reckless, courageous men who held unswerving loyalty to their master.

Their right hands were on the hilts of their curved sharp swords; in their left hands were the torches that lit the scene with a brightness that was near to daylight. By the way they stood, watching that crowd, they knew how ticklish was the moment — they knew that it needed little to set the mob storming against the confident, arrogant, miscalculating Nuhas, who had cost them so many lives only a few hours before. And they were ready to defend him to the death.

Tex began to force his way to the back of the crowd. There was work for him to do, if he was to save that column — and bonny Nicky — from eventual annihilation. He had to move fast, and disregard for the moment the circumstances leading to the capture of Suleiman.

But he was still trapped amid that throng when he heard Nuhas Pasha speak. He was a bold man, that former idol of the Arab world. He knew that his leadership was in question; knew that if he showed weakness and permitted a rival to step into his shoes then his life was assuredly forfeit, for that was the way things went in this savage Arab world of warlords.

The dilemma facing Nuhas was this: he

knew that Sheik Mahmoud was conspiring to oust him from leadership, and was only waiting for sign of support from the main host of Arab warriors before he struck. He knew this, knew that Mahmoud was the enemy; yet he had to pretend he didn't know, and had to defeat Mahmoud's plans without referring to that important sheik.

So now Nuhas Pasha stood up and spoke boldly and used crude psychology to keep the crowd with him.

What was this that he had heard from the lips of this ill-favoured dog? he demanded. Had he heard right, that one who was born an Arab should argue that a war against the accursed infidel Frank was wrong and should be ended immediately?

Nuhas drew himself up, mighty and majestic in his rich robes, and thundered: 'This wretch, this thing with evil written plain for men to see on his face, this man is a renegade, in the pay of our accursed enemies!'

And then he shouted: 'This man must die. That is my judgment!' At once men shouted with savage approval; for when men have suffered, whether in spirit or in body, they find satisfaction in witnessing the suffering of others and are without justice and reason in their choice of victim at these times.

Nuhas knew that a killing would take these primitive-minded men at least temporarily from the brooding that threatened his security — he knew mob psychology and employed it to the full.

He called, imperiously: 'Let this man die as he deserves. Let him die in pain, for he is as one with our enemies. And,' he added significantly, his words full of meaning and menace so that they quieted the crowd completely, 'let all men die in like manner who seek to upset Allah's chosen leaders in this war against the unfaithful. Roast him alive!'

A great, savage roar went up at that. Willing hands brought fire before the tent, poles were stabbed in on either side of it, with a long pole lashed horizontally between. Then Suleiman was hustled forward, struggling because even the calmest of men fight at the prospect of such a horrible death.

Tex, fighting his way back through the crowd, dragging that old, old Tormented Man with him, saw fierce, sadistic-minded Arabs swarm round the big Egyptian in his tattered cotton *galabier*, saw them drag Suleiman and tie him to that horizontal pole, his back to it, so that he faced down on to those smouldering embers only four feet below him. Then other eager sadists went plunging into the desert in search of scrub that would flame up — flame higher than a distance of four feet, say.

Tex fought his way through that mob, and no one seemed to notice the rough way he knocked men aside; for their eyes were on the spectacle of torture, and they had thoughts for nothing else at that moment.

Which was how the sagacious, cynical Nuhas Pasha had intended it. Suleiman was the victim who was to take the crowd's attention away from him, the unsuccessful war leader. And at the same time it was a bold warning for anyone to interpret . . . that this way men died who opposed the will of Allah.

At any rate, the will of Allah's self-chosen spokesmen, like Nuhas Pasha.

Back away from that crowd Tex looked round. He saw a knot of ragged men conferring, and knew them to be Tormented Men immediately.

The old, old man said: 'What is in your mind, my son?'

'For Suleiman? I would save him,' said Tex swiftly. Yes, save Suleiman though only two days before Suleiman had intended to kill him. But even before attending to Suleiman, he had to create the diversion that would bring in all the Arab troops and so leave the way clear for the hard-pressed, beleaguered French force to escape in the night.

And Nicky escape, of course. More to this man now than the lives of all those mercenary soldiers was the life of brave, blue-eyed, laughing-voiced Nicky Shaw the newspaperwoman from New York who wanted to quit news-reporting and settle on a ranch in Texas — with him.

He spoke rapidly, yet gave his instructions clearly. Would the Brotherhood of Tormented Men do as he asked? It was in

258

accordance with the aims of the Brethren, he assured that slow-thinking old Arab; this was a blow against the war leaders that Suleiman would surely approve of.

After what seemed minutes, the old, old man agreed that perhaps Suleiman would approve of the idea, especially now that Suleiman was beginning a torment that would end soon in death. Tex watched that ancient, wrinkled-faced Arab go across to his fellows. They conferred, hesitated, then melted into the darkness behind the tents.

Tex threw caution to the winds now. There was a crackling sound that spoke of tinder-dry brushwood being thrown on to those hot embers. Within seconds they would burst into flames and engulf Suleiman.

And suddenly Tex went crazy. Suddenly he couldn't bear the thought of that big ugly Arab being roasted into an agonising death. He disregarded completely the danger to himself in that desperate resolve to save the Tormented Man.

His arms swung before him, cleaving a pathway through the mass of startled tribesmen. Frantically he clawed his way through towards that open space, while startled Nuhas Pasha guards watched his approach and wondered.

Tex came to the edge of the crowd. A mighty Arab warrior stabbed warningly forward with his sword, to intimidate him into staying with the throng. Tex slipped under that outstretched arm, grabbed it by the wrist and hurled the warrior a clear fifteen yards across the open sand.

Then he went jumping forward, before anyone so much as thought to raise a gun against him. Nuhas Pasha was standing there amid his chiefs, astonishment on his face, for he had recognised in the legionnaire a man he had once met.

The smoke from the acrid smouldering brushwood burst into flame with the suddenness of a miniature explosion. Tex saw the eager licking tongues leap up to sear the skin of the choking, gasping Suleiman. Then his shoulder crashed into the pole support and sent the crude erection smashing on to the sand, away from the fire.

His knife was ripping through those

cords before the helpless Suleiman hit the sand. Then Tex's gun came out, menacing the Pasha. He was dragging Suleiman with him, towards the back of Nuhas Pasha's tent.

The mob was roaring, the guards jumping forward to strike down the bold intruder who had interrupted their sport. Then they stopped, aghast.

The back of Nuhas Pasha's tent suddenly blazed up in flames, that spoke of a saturation with palm oil. And by its fierce light they saw the two men, one dressed as an Arab, the other truly an Arab, for one instant silhouetted against the leaping flames . . .

Tex felt the gun clawed out of his hand. Saw Suleiman with it. Saw it pointing, and saw Nuhas Pasha with fear on his face, trying to escape retribution at the hands of the man he would have tortured to death. A shot rang out that could be heard even above the roaring of burning skins and precious carpets. Nuhas Pasha waltzed . . . and fell.

Tex grabbed Suleiman and they plunged through the burning back cloth, just as the whole tent whooshed into mighty flames. They came out, spitting and burning. Suleiman gave him back his revolver. Tex heard him say: 'That's one less to torment the world.' And he didn't feel like arguing against the crime.

All around them tents were burning — the whole Arab town was in flames. Tex saw men with torches still applying them to unburning goatskin tents, and knew this was the signal that the colonel would be looking for.

All around them men were riding in, aghast and wondering at the destruction. Then a shout went up that it was the work of Mahmoud's men, and the two factions flew to arms and began a battle of hate in the light of that blazing town of tents.

But Nuhas Pasha was dead; his followers were leaderless, and the ferocious Sheik Mahmoud, seeing his chance, began to drive his enemies back across the plain.

Tex pounded northwards; Suleiman, half-blind still from the smoky ordeal, stumbled along, gripping Tex's smouldering burnouse. Other Tormented Men saw them and joined them.

They ran on, while horsemen came tearing in from the darkness to join in the battle. They climbed. At length Tex reached the ridge.

It was deserted. The column had gone, perhaps only minutes before; and now was marching silently into the night. The tiny moon didn't help, didn't reveal the Legion or show their tracks in all that trampled disorder.

Tex looked north, to the east and to the west. They could be anywhere. Despair gripped him. He had saved the force from destruction, but now he had lost them, and lost contact with his comrades and Nicky, too.

He sat down on that ridge to await the coming of dawn, and the Brotherhood lay down beside him, perhaps to think that their first mission had not been entirely without success.

He fell asleep, exhausted. His last thought was that trying to find his friends in this mighty Sahara was like trying to find a needle in a haystack . . .

The first thing he saw when dawn came

to waken him was Nicky. She was asleep, about eighty yards away, curled up in a depression in the still-warm sand.

He got to his feet. The Brethren began to stir. All down that valley was chaos, with burnt-out tents and men lying in huddled death as far as he could see. The battle had raged beyond sight. Riderless horses stood by their dead masters. Tex thought: 'We'll need those . . . an' there'll be water in plenty in the skins on their saddles . . . '

Rube and Joe, tired-eyed from a long night's vigil, came up from a trench as they heard him approach. Their guns levelled as they saw that swirling bur-nouse. Then they recognised him, and came jumping forward in glad welcome. Nicky awoke and flew into his arms, sobbing with relief.

'She wouldn't go without you, Tex,' his comrades told him, patting him on the back as if they still couldn't believe their eyes. 'So we had to stay.'

Nicky said: 'I didn't trust those officers. I — I don't trust anyone except you and Rube and Good-looking here.' Joe smirked.

Nicky whispered: 'Is it all over?'

'All over,' said Tex, looking down that valley. 'We'll get hosses an' ride to the Valley-where-men-go-blind. I figger they'll give us Sturmer without any fuss now, those Tormented Men. I figger after last night I'm kinda taken into their brother-hood,' he drawled.

Suleiman heard him, Suleiman the Hideous . . . Suleiman the Enigma.

And as the legionnaires and bonny, blonde Nicky rode south with them later that morning, Suleiman was thinking that a man like Tex could be indispensable to the Brotherhood's plans to sweep the desert clear of Arab warmongers, tyrants — and the French.

THE END

We do hope that you have enjoyed reading this large print book.

Did you know that all of our titles are available for purchase?

We publish a wide range of high quality large print books including:
Romances, Mysteries, Classics
General Fiction
Non Fiction and Westerns

Special interest titles available in large print are:
The Little Oxford Dictionary
Music Book, Song Book
Hymn Book, Service Book

Also available from us courtesy of Oxford University Press:
Young Readers' Dictionary
(large print edition)
Young Readers' Thesaurus
(large print edition)

For further information or a free brochure, please contact us at:
Ulverscroft Large Print Books Ltd.,
The Green, Bradgate Road, Anstey,
Leicester, LE7 7FU, England.
Tel: (00 44) **0116 236 4325**
Fax: (00 44) **0116 234 0205**